'I chose you especially,' Sister Murphy sounded aggrieved, 'because you're the most efficient girl on the team. And I also thought that perhaps a morning's work with our charming new consultant might change your mind and persuade you to join the shift rota, *and* apply for the post of the second Sister we so badly need.'

'It would take a lot more charm and persuasion than Luke Roderick possesses to change my mind,' said Naomi, stepping out of the office.

'Pity,' the voice came from directly behind her.

Startled, Naomi spun round. 'It seems to be a habit you have of managing to overhear me,' she said icily.

'Seems to be a habit you have of taking offence,' he countered, eyes narrowed. 'Clock-watcher too!' The words were low, and far too quietly spoken for Sister Murphy to hear, but Naomi heard only too well, and her face flamed with suppressed fury.

'If that's what you care to think,' she replied, her voice equally low but pulsing with anger.

'Prove me wrong.'

Throwing caution to the winds, Naomi raised her voice, 'Mr Roderick, I don't have to *prove* anything to you!'

Ann Jennings has been married for thirty-two years and worked in a hospital for fourteen years—accounting for the technicalities accurately described in her hospital romances. Her son is a doctor and often provides her with amusing titbits of information. Hospitals are romantic places she maintains, romance blossoms where two people share a common interest.

Surgeon Ashore is Ann Jennings ninth Doctor Nurse Romance. Recent titles include *Nurse on Loan, Really, Doctor!* and *Sold to the Surgeon*.

SURGEON ASHORE

BY

ANN JENNINGS

MILLS & BOON LIMITED
ETON HOUSE   18-24 PARADISE ROAD
RICHMOND   SURREY   TW9 1SR

*All the characters in this book have no existence outside
the imagination of the Author, and have no relation
whatsoever to anyone bearing the same name or names.
They are not even distantly inspired by any individual
known or unknown to the Author, and all the incidents
are pure invention.*

*All Rights Reserved. The text of this publication or any
part thereof may not be reproduced or transmitted in
any form or by any means, electronic or mechanical,
including photocopying, recording, storage in an
information retrieval system, or otherwise, without the
written permission of the publisher.*

*This book is sold subject to the condition that it shall
not, by way of trade or otherwise, be lent, resold, hired
out or otherwise circulated without the prior consent of
the publisher in any form of binding or cover other than
that in which it is published and without a similar
condition including this condition being imposed on the
subsequent purchaser.*

*First published in Great Britain 1988
by Mills & Boon Limited*

© Ann Jennings 1988

*Australian copyright 1988
Philippine copyright 1988
This edition 1989*

ISBN 0 263 76333 1

*Set in Times 11 on 12 pt.
03 – 8902 – 51938*

Typeset in Great Britain by JCL Graphics, Bristol

Made and Printed in Great Britain.

CHAPTER ONE

'WHY NOT!' The words cut rapier-sharp through the air, slicing through the muted hubbub of murmuring voices, and stilling the crowded room into an awkward silence.

Staff Nurse Naomi Selborne drew herself up defiantly to her full height, a not inconsiderable five foot nine and stared at the man towering above her with barely ill concealed rancour. What right had he to dare question her motives? she thought crossly. It was none of his business if she chose not to apply for the Sister's post.

'Because I . . .' She hesitated momentarily, knowing with an instinctive certainty, even though she'd only just been introduced to Luke Roderick, the County General's new Consultant in Accident and Emergency, that he was not the type of man to be fobbed off with just any old excuse. A cursory scour of the corners of her brain for inspiration was without success. What she needed was a plausible excuse without actually revealing the real reason. But, unable to think of anything more elaborate, she just said quietly, but with a very definite emphasis on the words, 'Because I choose not to.'

Not a particularly original reason, she knew, but

one which could not be denied by anyone, especially not by the man quizzing her now. Prickling with resentment at the inquisition, she threw back her head defiantly, and the sun slanting through the window caught and lit up the streaks of gold in her hair, emphasising the echoing blaze in her tawny eyes.

'A lioness at bay.' The words were uttered so softly that later Naomi thought perhaps she had imagined them, as no one else seemed to have heard. More loudly he said, 'I see,' and the resonance of his deep voice echoed round the room. But to Naomi, although his tone was not unpleasant, the arrogant stance, long legs placed firmly apart, hands behind his back, said far more than the two words he'd just uttered.

Even allowing for her admitted prejudice—she had begun to bristle indignantly the moment he had started his inquisition—Naomi thought he oozed supreme self-assurance. As he moved, towering over everyone else in the room, it was easy to see he was used to looking down on people. Just being tall doesn't make you king of the castle, thought Naomi, feeling very rebellious. She didn't like this new sensation, she was used to looking most men straight in the eye because of her own height. But now, to her chagrin, where Luke Roderick was concerned she had no alternative but to look up like everyone else. It was absurd, she knew, but it made her feel ill at ease. It was just like being back at school, she reflected crossly, being reprimanded for some misdemeanour she'd committed.

Their eyes locked for a split second in silent battle, and Naomi felt her cheeks beginning to burn with a hot flush, but determinedly she kept her gaze steady. She was *not* going to be the first to look away. The amber flecks in her eyes sparkled with a challenging fire. I can, she thought doggedly, and will, outstare you any day; put that in your pipe and smoke it, Mr High and Mighty Luke Roderick! Involuntarily she tilted her head high in a subtle gesture of provocation, longing to say what was flashing through her mind, but not daring. Instead she had to be content with saying silently, I'm not the sort of girl you can bully, neither am I the sort to go weak at the knees, merely because you're tall, dark and very handsome, and so patently used to getting your own way!

'We'll discuss it later.' With an almost imperceptible movement of his muscular broad shoulders, he turned to the rest of the assembled company. Naomi drew a sharp breath. He'd shrugged her off as if to say he had more important things to deal with, and Nurse Selborne was a minor irritation, a wrinkle he'd iron out later!

'I think not, sir, my mind is made up.' Naomi snapped out the words, staccato and precise, noting with a small flicker of satisfaction the way his wide mouth clamped shut in a distinctly displeased line. A startled silence enveloped the room. Why, you could almost hear the proverbial pin drop, thought Naomi with some satisfaction; at last her point of view had well and truly registered!

Sister Murphy, taking advantage of the lull in the verbal sparring, which the rest of the staff had been observing with amazement, hurried forward, at the same time slanting a sideways glance at Naomi. She would never have believed it if she hadn't witnessed it with her own eyes. Staff Nurse Naomi Selborne had the reputation for being one of the quietest girls in A and E, and yet here she was almost having a stand-up row with their brand new consultant! Then her eyes swivelled in the direction of Luke Roderick, and immediately she forgot Naomi, as she surreptitiously hitched up her bra strap and tightened her belt in one swift movement. Enormous she might be, but like every other female Luke Roderick came into contact with, in no time at all she had quickly succumbed to his good looks and charm. Smiling broadly and touching his arm in a gesture of veneration, she drew him towards the other members of the Accident and Emergency Department gathered together in her tiny office.

Glad that the attention had at last switched from her, Naomi thankfully faded into relative obscurity at the back of the room. She squashed herself in by the side of her friend Gloria, who had yet to be introduced.

'Don't know why she's bothering with the belt and braces bit,' grinned Gloria wickedly, nodding in Sister's Murphy's direction. 'Somehow I don't think he's the type to go for sixteen stone and pebble-lensed glasses!'

Naomi suppressed a giggle. 'Anyway, he's probably married,' she whispered back, 'to some poor downtrodden little woman, and has a horde of nasty arrogant little children.'

'Wrong on both counts,' hissed Gloria. 'He's a bachelor, and as far as anyone knows childless!' Her whispered comments ended abruptly as her name was called, and she dutifully went forward to be introduced to the new boss.

Left alone, Naomi had the chance to covertly survey her inquisitor of the previous few minutes. He was intent on the other members of staff, and was not looking in her direction. With some degree of acrimony she surveyed his broad shoulders.

So this was the man Sister Murphy had been raving about all week. As Gloria had pointed out previously, anyone would think that she personally had been responsible for his appointment! Surgeon Luke Roderick was late of the Royal Navy, but more famous for his sailing adventures, the most recent of which had been presented as a lavish film on television. He was extremely tall, very dark, and good-looking in a hawkish kind of way. Naomi wrinkled her nose wryly. She must be the only member of the Accident and Emergency department who had not seen the epic adventure *Sinbad the Surgeon*, a recreation of the Arabian Nights tale of Sinbad the Sailor. She couldn't help thinking that A and E at the County General would seem pretty dull in comparison to those sun-filled sailing days, and the attendant glamour of film-making. Idly Naomi wondered why he had chosen to give up a successful career as a doctor-cum-TV star for the more mundane world of orthodox medicine.

As if in answer to her unspoken thoughts, she heard him replying to a question from Swaroop Rao, their pretty little Indian nurse. 'I decided I'd been self-indulgent long enough. It was time to join the real workers, the people in a busy district general hospital, like this one.' He waved his hands in an expansive gesture including everyone in the room. The staff exchanged delighted glances, all caught by the charisma of his flashing smile.

Everyone except Naomi, who for a reason she couldn't even logically explain to herself, was grimly determined not to fall under his spell. As she stared, his head turned in her direction, and she hastily looked away, but not before she caught sight of an amused glint in the depths of his eyes. She had been cramming her size seven foot into her size six shoe, and he, damn the wretched man, had noticed! Naomi hated her big feet, her only admission to vanity. She never bought shoes large enough, preferring instead to cripple herself by determinedly squeezing her feet into shoes a size too small.

She glanced at her watch, and breathed a soft sigh of relief. Thank goodness it was nearly time for her to leave and go home. The blissful thought displaced all others. Even the tightness of her shoes was forgotten. The whole room, including the daunting figure of Luke Roderick, was eclipsed, as a mental picture of Toby flashed before her inward eye. Soon he would be swinging backwards and forwards on the rickety gate as he waited for her, his socks, woolly concertinas around his ankles, defying Aunt Flo's rigorous efforts with elastic garters to keep them up. By his side would be Stubbs, her springer spaniel, his liver and white feathery coat bedraggled with mud from the saltings. A tender smile curved her full lips at the thought of the ecstatic, if rather muddy, welcome she would receive from them both.

'Sister tells me it's time for you to go now. I hadn't realised you worked part-time.' A voice ringing with sarcasm slashed across her pleasantly meandering thoughts, bringing her back to reality with a disagreeable jolt.

'I don't call thirty-five and a half hours a week part-time.' Inclining her head proudly, she looked up, and once more their eyes locked in conflict. He might as well get used to the idea, thought Naomi crossly, that one member of his staff was not impressed by his star status.

'Thirty-five and a half—I see we're being pedantic!'

'Not we, *you*!' Without glancing in his direction again, although powerfully aware that he had taken an involuntary step towards her at her scornful reply, Naomi turned towards Sister Murphy. 'May I go now, Sister?'

'Er . . . certainly, Nurse Selborne,' Sister said after a slight hesitation.

Huh! she doesn't want to upset darling Mr Roderick, thought Naomi disdainfully, noting the hesitation, and contemptuous of the fact that Sister Murphy was so obviously fawning at the new consultant's feet.

Leaving the room quickly, and trying to glide out in what she hoped were cool, seemingly unhurried steps, although her legs felt obstinately wooden, she glanced surreptitiously back. A sea of rapt faces was gazing up at the dark imperious figure of Luke Roderick, all of them listening intently. As if every word he uttered was forged of pure gold, she thought disapprovingly. Never mind, they'd soon learn. He was no different from anyone else, in spite of his exploits. Now he was just another doctor working in A and E.

Passing the main reception desk, she was halted in her tracks by Paula Scott and Richard Nicholas. Paula, the receptionist, and Richard, one of the registrars, had been left to man the department in the absence of the rest of the staff. They were both bemoaning the fact that they were missing all the excitement.

'What excitement?' Naomi queried in answer to their questions. 'He's only a new consultant, and we've all seen plenty of them before.'

'Ah yes, but not one who's so sexy, and a TV star,' moaned Paula. Sighing heavily, she propped her elbows on the desk and cupped her chin in her hands. 'Sinbad the Surgeon,' she murmured dreamily.

'Huh, I can see I'm not going to get a look in with any of the girls now,' said Richard gloomily, as he too leaned beside Paula.

Naomi burst out laughing. 'What a pair you look—the picture of misery!' Reaching out, she gently banged their heads together. 'You've got nothing to worry about, Richard,' she said, 'because Paula will very soon discover that he's not nearly as sexy as she thinks, just an ordinary man.' But even as she uttered the words an uncomfortable little niggle at the back of her mind reminded her that she was not being strictly honest!

'It's true, and it's no laughing matter,' protested Richard.

'Don't worry about him, he's old enough to be Paula's father. Luke Roderick's not dangerous to the opposite sex, he's . . .'

'I wouldn't count on that, Nurse. I *can* be dangerous, very dangerous indeed!'

With a simultaneous stifled gasp, the three of them whirled round to face in the direction of the dark brown voice.

'But I thought . . .' faltered Naomi, embarrassed at being caught gossiping, especially by the man in question.

'That I was still in the office!' he finished the sentence on a mocking note. 'Well, as you can see for yourself, I am not—and before you go,' he added as Naomi took a hasty step towards the swing doors which lay between her and the outside world, 'perhaps I ought to tell you that in spite of my advanced years, I'm very alert! Not much escapes my notice.' He paused, and Naomi felt herself blushing bright pink as his gaze lingered

quite deliberately on the slender lines of her body.
'Just remember I'm not in my dotage yet!'

Unable to think of an appropriate reply, Naomi
fled, her cheeks burning, and they burned even
more as the sound of his sudden laughter echoed
after her. Her face was still scarlet when she
reached the car park, and located her dilapidated
old Renault. Why is it, she thought, fumbling with
her car keys in the lock, I can never think of witty
or scathing replies when I need them? I bet I think
of something sensational in the bath tonight!

In spite of her defiant words earlier, telling
Paula and Richard he was only a new consultant,
there were ominous rumblings deep in her
subconscious. Vaguely and quite irrationally she
felt that the new surgeon was destined to be a
disruptive influence. She fervently hoped that any
disruptions he caused would be confined to the
hospital department, and not spill over into her
private life.

Logic and plain old-fashioned common sense
told her she was being stupid, nevertheless Naomi
couldn't shake off the slightly uneasy, jittery mood
that enveloped her as she wrestled with the snaggle
of evening traffic streaming out from the city. It
was a feeling she didn't manage to banish until she
drove the car up the tree-shaded lane beside
Longstone church, and saw Toby, untidy as ever,
swinging on the gate, just the way she'd imagined,
the sturdy shape of a very muddy springer spaniel
sitting beside him.

Home at last, and the feeling of anxiety

dissipated like magic in the dappled sunlight of the lane, where the only confusion was in the tangled mass of dog-roses competing for every inch of space in the hedgerow. Now the disturbing memory of Luke Roderick could be packed neatly away into the recesses of her mind and forgotten. Although why on earth she should think of him as disturbing she just couldn't imagine. He was only another man, a doctor in the department. With the perspective of distance she was able to tell herself she had overreacted, and was probably doing the poor man a great injustice.

Hugging Toby, who was trying to tell her half a dozen things about school at once, and vainly trying to fend off the muddy paws of an over-enthusiastic Stubbs, she forgot about Luke, concentrating instead on her joy at being home for the weekend.

Aunt Flo, Toby's guardian from Monday to Friday, was in the kitchen, surrounded by a glistening mountain of mixed fruit from the garden. She paused for a moment from her task of topping and tailing the gooseberries and blew Naomi a sticky kiss.

'Pot of tea and fresh baked scones over there, dear,' she said, nodding in the direction of the Aga. 'I must finish this jam—we'll eat later.'

Stopping to kiss Aunt Flo's apple-smooth cheek, Naomi kicked off her too tight shoes, thankfully slipping her feet into a sloppy old pair of espadrilles. Then she subsided gratefully into the capacious leather armchair by the window.

A delicious aroma of boiling jam permeated the room, mixed in with the more tangy odour of the soused herrings cooling at the other end of the scrubbed pine table. Here, the hard slog of Monday to Friday seemed light years away, something that happened on another planet. Now Naomi was in her other world, her *real* world.

The weekend flashed past far too quickly. It was gone in a golden haze of walks along the beach, swimming, feeding the gulls and helping Aunt Flo. But even as she luxuriated in every moment, Naomi knew the enchanted world she'd nurtured so carefully over the last few years couldn't last for ever. Watching Toby play a game of tag with Stubbs on the beach, their last few moments together before she had to return to the bed-sit she occupied near the County General, she wished, not for the first time, that Tiffany had lived to see her son.

Tiffany, her lovely, wayward, headstrong elder sister, who had died giving birth to Toby, leaving Naomi, twenty-one years old and newly qualified as a nurse, to take on the responsibility of rearing the orphaned Toby. Apart from widowed Aunt Flo, there had been no one else, no one else to shoulder the burden.

At the very beginning Naomi had felt resentful. Tiffany hadn't even been able to tell her the name of Toby's father, because she had died before Naomi had managed to reach the remote cottage hospital in Wales she had sped to in answer to an urgent summons. As she watched Toby play, her lips curved in a sad smile as she remembered the shock it had been to find that Tiffany was about to give birth. No one had even known she was pregnant, and it was even worse that she had died leaving behind a fatherless child.

For a moment the familiar uncomfortable guilty feeling stirred in the deep recesses of her heart—'Father unknown'. That was not strickly true. Naomi had always had a pretty shrewd idea who the father was. Tiffany's one constant companion in the preceding months had been Dirk Roderigues, a formula one racing driver, and now world champion for three consecutive years. Naomi had met him several times; he had been younger than Tiffany, highly strung and emotional, with a reputation for being totally reckless on and off the race track. At first she'd worried, and had been tempted to get in touch with him. But then, when he failed to contact her, she'd dismissed the idea. How did one go up to a man, practically a stranger, and say, 'I think my sister had your son!'

She had smothered any feelings of guilt by telling herself that Dirk appeared to have forgotten that Tiffany had ever existed. His name was linked quite soon after Toby's birth with that of another model, and then another, and another, and his reputation for being an 'enfant terrible' increased as he nearly killed himself, time after time, at each exotic Grand Prix location.

Naomi had hardened her heart against him when

she'd read of his exploits. Poor Tiffany, she had
thought bitterly, she had sped through life with the
brilliance of a shooting star, only to burn out and
disappear for ever as shooting stars always do,
leaving one small bright spark behind her, a small
boy named Toby.

It had only taken a few short weeks for that
small bright spark to worm his way into Naomi's
tender heart, and soon she hadn't wanted to know
who his father was. She didn't want to share Toby
with anyone, except Aunt Flo.

'Let sleeping dogs lie,' had been Aunt Flo's
advice, and rightly or wrongly she'd taken it. And
that was the way they'd both liked it.

Of course there had been a price to pay. As an
attractive girl, Naomi was surprisingly short of
men friends. She'd soon found out that the male of
the species usually beat a hasty retreat when they
discovered she had a small boy in tow, more
particularly as he was very much a permanent
feature of her life.

Not that she minded now, Naomi was
independent and determined. Her main aim in life
was to provide for Toby; hence her rather
unorthodox fixed working hours. A nurse's pay
wasn't sufficient income to pay for the private
school Toby would attend in a few years' time,
where he would have to be a boarder. Aunt Flo
wasn't getting any younger, and although she
coped at the moment, both she and Naomi knew
the day would come when the burden would prove
too much. Naomi, being the realist she was, didn't

believe in letting the grass grow under her feet and worked steadily for the future.

During the week, the moment she was off duty at the hospital she changed like a chameleon into her other life. She was a waitress four nights a week at an exclusive local restaurant, The Water's Edge. Every penny she earned from waitressing was carefully put away towards Toby's school fees.

The hard work didn't worry her, although by the time every Friday arrived she was exhausted, and people making sarcastic remarks about working to suit herself irritated her. She winced suddenly, as she recalled Luke Roderick's words as clearly as if he were beside her. Working part-time indeed! If only he knew!

But he didn't and wouldn't. No one at the hospital knew, not even Gloria who was the closest to being her best friend. That was another drawback, working such long hours left no time for socialising, and Naomi had the reputation of being a bit of a recluse.

Monday morning duly arrived, and as she came out of the nurses' changing room the first sight that met Naomi's eyes was Luke Roderick. He was striding purposefully down the corridor, white coat tails flying like sails in the wind, the set of his shoulders emanating strength and determination.

No, I think it is *definitely* better not to get on the wrong side of him, thought Naomi, making a mental note to steer as clear of the man in question as was humanly possible, reasoning that as she had not exactly got off to a brilliant start on Friday, there was no point in putting herself in the way of any flak that might be flying.

Unfortunately, however, for Naomi, Sister Murphy had other ideas. She came lumbering officiously down the corridor, all sixteen stone of her, her belt pulled in so tight, she looked as if she would pop if anyone stuck a pin in her.

'I've put you down to help Mr Roderick with his first referral clinic,' she said, handing Naomi the week's rota. 'We've discussed the allocation of duties, and he's pleased with my ideas.' Her ample bosom puffed up even more as she uttered the word 'we'.

Naomi felt the same irrational irritation she'd felt on Friday. Luke Roderick had obviously used his charms to good advantage where Sister Murphy was concerned. She had thought then that he was a practised charmer. It was something she could never fathom out, why it was that so many women always fell hook, line and sinker for that type of man. That false magic never worked for her, perhaps because Tiffany had been let down by such a man Naomi was always wary.

So it was with a degree of reluctance that she took the proffered rota. She would have much preferred to have started the week off with anyone other than Luke Roderick, but short of causing a problem first thing on Monday morning, there was nothing she could do.

'I'll make sure everything for the clinic is ready,' was her only comment as she hurried away in the direction of the referral clinic.

The morning referral clinic was held every day in an area tacked on to the side of the main Casualty area. The list of patients had already been typed and was pinned to the wall—forty cases in all.

'Yes, a damned busy weekend,' said Richard Nicholas, coming up behind her, taking off his white coat as he spoke and stuffing it into the dirty linen bin. 'Seventy-two hours on duty, and four hours' sleep. I feel knackered!'

'And look it,' said Naomi sympathetically, looking at his haggard unshaven face. 'Why don't you go now before you get nabbed by the new consultant. Sam Brice is already here. I saw him chatting up Paula when I came through.' Sam was the duty senior house officer about to take over.

'Huh, all right for some,' grumbled Richard, 'I never have the time or energy to chat up anybody!'

'My heart bleeds for you,' teased Naomi, knowing full well that after a few hours' sleep, Richard would probably be his usual irrepressible self, particularly where young and pretty females were concerned.

'Take pity on a poor, unloved and lonely registrar,' groaned Richard in mock agony, slipping an arm around Naomi's slim waist. 'What are your plans tonight?'

'Your plans, Dr Nicholas, should involve being back here on duty, unless I'm very much mistaken,' snapped a deep voice behind them.

They sprang apart with a guilty jump, and Naomi nervously smoothed an imaginary crease from the skirt of her immaculate uniform. Oh dear, she'd been so determined to start the morning off with a calm efficient air. Oh well, she thought morosely, the death knell was well and truly sounded for that faint hope!

Luke Roderick's next words merely added to her gloom. 'If you're feeling that energetic, Nurse, then I'm sure you won't mind working late tonight. I understand we're one down owing to sickness.'

'I'm sorry, sir, but I'm afraid I can't.' Swallowing her frustration at being manoeuvred into the wrong in his eyes yet again, Naomi picked up the pile of case notes and walked through to the consulting room.

Catching his gaze as she turned, she was surprised to see a strange mixture of amusement and something else lurking in the depths of his eyes. Her back suddenly bristled with indignation, ramrod-stiff. Why, he had done it on purpose! He had baited her with a proposal he knew very well she'd refuse. Shooting him a malevolent glare, she stalked out of the room. The man was nothing but a sadist!

CHAPTER TWO

PROFESSIONALISM and training rose to the fore, however, and swallowing the resentment that rose in her throat at being disadvantaged yet again by an astute tactical move on Luke Roderick's part, Naomi tried to forget it and concentrate on the patients.

Clasping the first set of case notes, she surveyed the patients sitting in orderly rows on the waiting room chairs. She'd already scanned the list and seen that most of them were pretty minor things, the major cases having been admitted as inpatients on to the wards. But Naomi knew that just these cases alone would have been enough to keep Richard on the run the whole weekend, and that was discounting the majors he'd had to admit.

The first patient she ushered into the consulting room was a case of sunburn. The young man in question had been foolish enough to go sailing most of the weekend without a shirt. He was a pale-skinned Londoner, now burnt to a frazzle.

'I'll know next time, Nurse,' he said, wincing as Naomi helped him off with his shirt. 'A cool sea breeze lulled me into a false sense of security.'

'You're not the first to make that mistake,' Naomi consoled him.

'The young doctor I saw yesterday morning gave me some cream, but it hasn't cured it.'

Naomi smiled at the surprise in his voice. Like most patients, he seemed to think doctors had magic potions to cure everything! 'I'm afraid there's no quick cure, you'll have to . . .'

'Thank you, Nurse, I'll take over. Notes, please,' Cutting through her words, Luke Roderick breezed in and took the case notes from her hand.

Biting her lip, Naomi moved aside. A case of 'you big white doctor, me slave', she thought, feeling cross. He might have had the courtesy to let her finish the sentence! But in spite of her mutinous thoughts, she stood back demurely, keeping silent and trying to look as if butter wouldn't melt in her mouth. He'd already had one dig at her that morning, and she certainly wasn't going to give him the opportunity for any more. If he wanted to play the big chief, Naomi determined she would be the last person to stand in his way!

She watched as he expertly examined the patient, quietly reprimanded him for being so stupid, then sent him grumbling on his way. Collecting the next file, she turned to go, when suddenly she became aware that his deep-set eyes were scrutinising her. It was a disconcerting feeling, as if she was being examined by a powerful microscope. Illogically, and much to her annoyance, she found herself wondering if her lipstick was smudged, or her hair had escaped from the confines of her cap—not the sort of thing that normally she would have thought twice about. 'I don't know what you've been doing this weekend, but it has most definitely done you good. You look positively blooming, not at all like the jaded girl of last Friday,' he grinned suddenly.

'Thanks for the backhanded compliment,' retorted Naomi, and found herself grinning back at him. It was true, and she knew it. She always felt different after her weekends with Toby and Aunt Flo. She felt rested and invigorated, her batteries recharged ready for the next week of hard slogging. But a compliment, even one with a slight sting in the tail, was something she hadn't expected from Luke Roderick of all people, and suddenly to her vexation she felt the warmth of a blush begin to steal across her cheeks.

Still he regarded her with a mesmerising stare which kept her rooted to the spot. 'Blushing suits you too, Naomi,' he announced finally, as if it was a scientific discovery.

It added to her surprise, hearing him use her first name. The unfamiliar use of the name Naomi startled her. The staff only ever called each other by their first names when they were well out of Sister's earshot.

'Sister Murphy prefers surnames, sir,' she said stiffly.

'I've told Rose—that's Sister Murphy's name, you know—that although I intend to run a very tight ship, I also intend it to be friendly. First names are the order of the day.'

Naomi raised her eyebrows. Tight ship indeed! It reminded her of his nautical origins, and she couldn't resist a cheeky 'Aye, aye, sir' as she left the room to collect the next patient.

The rest of the morning was frantically busy, leaving no time for small talk, or the friendly use of first names—for which Naomi was absurdly thankful. Somehow she couldn't envisage herself calling the rather forbidding man she was working with by his first name.

'Luke,' she tried it experimentally under her breath—but couldn't bring herself to say it out loud. But she noticed that although he had said he wanted to be wanted to be friendly, it only needed one small thing out of place, or a fraction of a second's delay, and his penetrating glower was anything but friendly!

Gloria didn't help matters by making repeated entrances with notes she'd ostensibly forgotten to put in the pile, although Naomi knew well enough it was all in an effort to get herself noticed by Luke. But even she quailed after being told sharply that perhaps she should take a special course in memory improvement! Instead of sliding out of the door with her usual sexy wiggle, she had positively scuttled, and Naomi had smothered a grin. Poor Gloria, she had tried so hard to get Luke to notice the glamour girl of the department, and so he had, but not quite in the way she had intended!

Naomi, however, was basically a generous-hearted girl, and had to give credit where it was due. It didn't take her long to decide that there was no doubt that Luke Roderick was an extremely good and conscientious doctor. Every patient was made to feel that they could take as long as they liked, and that their injury, no matter how minor, was his major concern.

She watched as he gained the confidence of a small girl who needed her sutured lip examined.

'Emma won't let you look at it,' said the child's mother with a triumphant air. 'Why, she wouldn't even let *me* go near it.'

But Luke soon had the little girl gazing up at him, eyes as big as saucers, as he told her wild and wonderful tales of Sinbad's sailors. Particularly about one who, according to Luke, had just such an injury as Emma. 'Only he wasn't nearly as brave as you,' he said.

'He wasn't?' lisped Emma.

I must ask him when he last kissed the Blarney Stone, thought Naomi, listening with wry amusement to the unlikely tale he was spinning the little girl. But it did the trick. Emma happily let him swab the suture clean of the remnants of congealed blood so that he could inspect it, and then went off clutching her 'bravery medal' which Luke solemnly presented to her when it was all finished.

Naomi smiled at the badge Emma showed her. It said 'I Love Doctors' in bright red letters. 'Yes, it's lovely,' she said dutifully in answer to Emma's enquiring look.

Mother and daughter left the room, and Luke pulled open the drawer of his desk. 'Job lot,' he said, raising one dark eyebrow. 'You'd be surprised how useful they are. Why, sometimes I even persuade nurses to wear them!' His eyes sparkled with a wicked gleam, and suddenly Naomi was reminded of the pictures of buccaneers in storybooks.

'Yes, I thought you must have given Sister Murphy one of those this morning!' she retorted acidly, overreacting against the alluring glitter of his eyes. All he needed, she thought wryly, was a gold earring and a sabre to rattle, and he'd be the perfect hero for any swashbuckling pirate film.

But far from being annoyed at her acrimonious reply, he merely laughed. 'I've always found it a good policy to get the Sisters on my side,' he said. 'Nurses too,' he added softly as Naomi departed to collect the last patient.

She stopped dead, and turned to stare at him. 'I'm on the side of the patients,' she snapped. He really was the most aggravating man, he spoke as if having all the nurses adore him was something he expected as a matter of course!

The final patient, a William Thomas, shambled across the lengthy expanse of the waiting room area when Naomi called his name. She waited, wishing he would hurry. Her feet were killing her, and she thought with longing of the canteen where she could kick off her shoes and relax. Gloria was forever nagging her to get bigger shoes, but Naomi was stubbornly obstinate on the score. There was nothing she could do about her height, but at least she could *appear* to have small feet, even if it did mean half killing herself in the process.

'Don't know why I've had to come back,'

muttered the lanky youth when he finally joined her. 'I had an X-ray early this morning, and the doc said everything was OK.'

'A routine check by a senior consultant,' Naomi told him, 'just to make quite sure nothing was missed.'

'How can you miss anything on an X-ray?'

'You'd be surprised,' said Naomi, never dreaming how prophetically true her words were.

Passing the notes across the desk to Luke, she clipped the X-rays on to the small desk-mounted screen before him, and then stood back. It was the last case of the morning. They were running late, but not too late. A glance at her watch told her that at least she'd manage a reasonable lunch break.

'Who saw this patient?' Luke's brusque voice snapped her wandering thoughts back on target.

'Why . . . er . . . Dr Nicholas, I expect.' Naomi checked the admission notes, sure enough Richard's large illegible writing sprawled untidily across the page.

There was an ominous silence as Luke carefully studied the X-rays again. He didn't say anything, he didn't need to, he was bristling with anger and annoyance, and Naomi's heart slumped to the bottom of her too-tight shoes. Oh dear, trouble ahead, she thought gloomily.

When he finally did speak his voice vibrated with displeasure. 'There's a fractured scaphoid here, and it's been missed.'

Naomi moved round and peered over his shoulder, following the direction of his pointing finger. Sure enough, the thin line of fracture on the tiny scaphoid bone in the wrist was there. To an untrained eye the X-ray looked normal, but Naomi could see it. There was no doubt about it, the scaphoid was fractured.

She felt a pang of compassion for Richard Nicholas. Luke wasn't the type to tolerate mistakes, poor Richard would be for the high jump. Glancing down at the admission notes, she noticed that the time of admission was two-thirty that morning, near the end of Richard's long stint of very busy duty. He would have been tired, and it was an easy fracture to miss. Perhaps Luke would take that into consideration, and go easy on him.

'Nurse, take Mr Thomas to the plaster room immediately.' The friendly use of first names appeared to have been forgotten, she noticed as he furiously scribbled instructions to the plaster technician.' And I want to see the patient again, once he's plastered.'

Although surprised at the request—consultants didn't normally see patients straight away after plastering—Naomi remained silent. But some of her surprise must have shown on her face, as he turned and answered her unspoken question.

'I want to be absolutely certain that the thumb is in the correct position. That's essential, if an adequate blood supply to the scaphoid is to be maintained.'

'Yes, sir,' murmured Naomi, ushering the slightly bemused patient towards the door. She was tempted to say that their excellent plaster technician had probably plastered more fractured scaphoids than Luke Roderick had had hot dinners, but reflected grimly that the less said at the moment the better!

William Thomas grumbled all the way down the long scubbed corridor towards the plaster room. 'Wish I hadn't come in now,' he muttered ungratefully. 'I wished I'd stayed in bed and had an extra hour's kip.'

Naomi said nothing, resolutely maintaining a forbearing silence with difficulty—although his next words caused her to break that resolution.

'It was me mates who made me come to the hospital, after we got back from the party. I told them I was OK, had been ever since I fell over in the pub at six o'clock,' he giggled foolishly. He's still suffering from the after-effects of drink, thought Naomi angrily.

'Do you mean to tell me you waited from six o'clock in the evening until two-thirty in the morning before you came in?' she demanded incredulously. 'Don't you realise how tired the night duty staff are by the early hours of the morning? Two-thirty should be kept for *real* emergencies.'

'I am a *real* emergency,' he answered truculently. 'The doctor I've just seen made that plain enough.' He sniggered, and Naomi longed to cuff him around his rather protruding red ears. 'That young doc I saw this morning is going to cop it, isn't he? Right bloomer he made. Perhaps I should sue.'

'I wouldn't advise it.' Naomi's tone was glacial. 'The fracture has been identified now, that's what referral clinics are for.' She was astounded at the nerve of the unpleasant youth—fancy even suggesting that he should sue! But she was sure that Luke Roderick would stand behind Richard in such an unlikely event.

As for William Thomas, he opened his mouth to reply, but seeing Naomi's uncompromisingly stern look, thought better of it and kept silent. It was a silence he maintained during the plastering, and on the way back to the consulting room. The vibes that she could have cheerfully throttled him seemed to have penetrated through his thick skull.

Once the patient was back in the consulting room, a quick glance satisfied Luke that all was well, and he sent the thoughtless youth on his way. The X-ray was still on the illuminated screen, and Naomi took a deep breath and decided to grasp the bull by the horns. Looking at Luke before she began to speak, she thought what a very apt metaphor it was. He was certainly looking rather bullish, his huge shoulders hunched over the desk in a bad-tempered way.

'Dr Nicholas had been on duty for nearly seventy-two hours when this case came in,' she ventured.

'So?' he snapped.

'So, he was tired,' continued Naomi, determined to make her point, 'and after only four hours' sleep in seventy-two, a scaphoid fracture is an easy one to miss.'

'Doctors are trained not to miss things. Dr Nicholas knew, when he took up medicine, that the hours are long and arduous. Unlike nurses, junior doctors can't pick and choose their hours, and he knows that.'

'But Richard . . .' Naomi flushed at the pointed reference to her own working hours, but tried to continue in her friend's defence.

'Your concern for Dr Nicholas is touching,' clipped sarcasm laced the words with sharpness, 'but hardly any of your business, even if he is one of your boyfriends.' With a quick movement he picked up the single sheaf of notes remaining on his desk and thrust them into her hands in a clearly dismissive gesture.

Naomi opened her mouth to reply, then closed it again. It was quite obvious she would only be wasting her breath. 'Yes, Mr Roderick,' she confined herself to saying as she turned on her heel.

'Luke,' he corrected.

I prefer Mr Roderick, thought Naomi mutinously. Luke sounded far too friendly, and friendliness was the one emotion she was most definitely *not* harbouring at that moment! A good doctor he might be, but he was proving to be unreasonable where his own junior staff were concerned, something Naomi thought unfair. So gathering up the rest of the case notes, and ignoring his last remark, she made her exit in frigid silence.

Her black mood persisted as she started to make

her way down to the canteen, situated in the bowels
of the hospital. She had to pass Sister Murphy's
office, and she was sitting there, eating the mound
of sandwiches she always brought in for her lunch,
her nose buried between the pages of a paperback
novel, which had a lurid picture of a dark pirate
spread across the front cover.

On hearing Naomi's footsteps, Sister looked up.
'how did you get on with Luke this morning?' She
let the name Luke roll around her tongue.

She's savouring the imaginary intimacy, thought
Naomi cynically, and wondered if Sister Murphy
had noticed the resemblance between the new
consultant and the picture of the piratical hero of
her novel.

Reluctant, however, to waste any of her precious
lunch break, she paused only briefly in the
doorway. 'OK,' she said noncommittally. She
didn't want to get involved in a long discussion.

Sister Murphy snapped her book shut and placed
it on the desk top, one pudgy hand covering the
front cover as she regarded Naomi with some
asperity.

She's flattened her dearly beloved, thought
Naomi irreverently, stifling a sudden desire to
giggle. Sister's penchant for lurid gothics was well
known, and a constant source of amusement
amongst the nurses.

'I chose you especially,' Rose Murphy sounded
aggrieved, 'because you're the most efficient girl
on the team.' She paused for a moment, then
added, 'And I also thought that perhaps a

morning's work with our charming new consultant might change your mind and persuade you to join the shift rota, *and* apply for the post of the second Sister we so badly need.' She sighed heavily. 'Goodness knows, the work is piling up, especially the paperwork.'

Tempted though she was to point out that if Sister refrained from reading her perpetual supply of books and did some of the paperwork herself, things wouldn't get so far behind, Naomi merely said mildly, 'I'm afraid I haven't changed my mind.'

'But Luke is so charming, so persuasive, I thought . . .'

'It would take a lot more charm and persuasion than Luke Roderick possesses to change my mind,' said Naomi, stepping out of the office. She glanced quickly at her watch—damn, fifteen minutes of her lunch break gone already!

'Pity,' the voice came from directly behind her.

Startled, Naomi spun round. 'It seems to be a habit you have of managing to overhear me,' she said icily.

'Seems to be a habit you have of taking offence,' he countered, eyes narrowed. Was it annoyance or laughter? Naomi couldn't be sure, but it had the effect of making her feel nervously guilty. His voice changed, adopting a bantering pleading note. 'Can't I make you reconsider concerning the Sister's post?'

'Certainly not!' snapped Naomi, nervousness making her sound far more emphatic than she had intended. 'Once I've made up my mind, it stays made up. Now, if you'll excuse me . . .'

She paused, waiting for him to step back out of her way, but he remained where he was, passive, but very effectively blocking her way with the bulk of his body. Naomi glowered. At this rate the whole of her precious lunch hour was going to disappear. There was no alternative but to squeeze past, so with a sizzling flash of anger spitting flame from her golden eyes, she manoeuvred herself through the doorway.

Her slim body brushed against his chest, ruffling the crisp white coat, and she was suddenly conscious of a crazy tumult of mixed emotions rushing through her, like a mass of flotsam in flood water. It was as if she had touched a high-voltage cable. Startled, and suddenly breathless, she glanced up involuntarily towards him, only to find his eyes regarding her with an impenetrable expression, his mouth curved with the merest hint of mocking amusement.

'Clock-watcher too!'

The words were low, and far too quietly spoken for Sister Murphy to hear, but Naomi heard only too well, and her face flamed with suppressed fury.

'If that's what you care to think,' she replied, her voice equally low but pulsing with anger.

'Prove me wrong.'

Throwing caution to the winds, Naomi raised her voice. 'Mr Roderick, I don't have to *prove* anything to you!'

Lips tight, head held high, she strode away, not

waiting to hear if there was a reply. Although she
had no doubt he could have thought of something
suitably insulting. Charming and persuasive
indeed! Sister Rose Murphy must be wearing
glasses tinted to match her name! Luke Roderick,
she decided angrily, was about as charming and
persuasive as a cobra!

CHAPTER THREE

ANGER speeding her footsteps as she hurried down the corridor for her belated lunch, Naomi was well aware of two pairs of eyes following her progress—Those of Luke Roderick, and those of Sister Murphy. Her eyes were as round as an owl's behind her horn-rimmed spectacles, although whether it was from horror at Naomi's last words, which she must surely have overheard, or whether it was because she was busily trying to stuff the paperback novel surreptitiously into her drawer, Naomi was uncertain.

The only thing she was absolutely certain about was that she had annoyed their new consultant yet again. It seemed she had a flair for doing that. But equally, reflected Naomi grimly, her gentle mouth tightening into a stern line at the thought, he also seemed to have the perfect knack for making her hackles rise, *and,* she was sure, took a perverse delight in doing so. If I were a dog, she thought resentfully, quickening her pace along the corridor, he'd have the hairs on my back standing on end! Then she grinned suddenly at the ridiculous notion. Why, if I were a dog, she concluded, I would have bitten him by now!

Immersed in her thoughts, and rapidly gathering

speed along the polished floor leading towards the canteen, she failed to see Richard until she'd cannoned straight into him.

'Luke Roderick wants to see you,' she told him, thinking she might as well warn him of the potential danger.

'Oh, crumbs, what have I done now?' Richard groaned wearily his eyes still dull from lack of sleep.

When Naomi told him about the missed scaphoid fracture, he clasped his hands to his head and groaned even louder. Then turning back towards the direction of Casualty, he started down the corridor. 'Might as well get the beating, metaphorically speaking, over and done with,' he said philosophically, shrugging his shoulders.

'Don't forget to remind him you only had four hours' sleep,' said Naomi.

'Do you honestly think it will make any difference?'

'Well, actually no . . .' said Naomi truthfully, then she tried to smile encouragingly. 'But there's no harm in telling him, he might be understanding. It's worth a try.'

'And pigs might fly!' came back the gloomy response, as Richard trudged off with a martyr's air of fated resignation.

Later that afternoon, during a break between cases, Richard caught up with Naomi and Gloria sneaking a quick coffee in the little office just off Casualty, which served as a coffee-cum-rest room.

'Actually Luke wasn't as bad as I'd expected,' he

told them, pouring himself a black coffee. 'He said it was a difficult fracture to spot, and gave me some useful pointers. Although he did add that he wouldn't tolerate another mistake.' He pulled a face, and added as an afterthought, 'But I didn't need to mention that I'd been up all night—he already knew.'

'You see, he *has* got a heart after all,' said Gloria triumphantly. She had been most put out when Naomi had told her that, in her opinion, Luke was a hard-hearted unfeeling man where his staff were concerned. She couldn't believe that anyone who looked so gorgeous could be anything less than godlike in their approach to life! Gloria and Naomi had always differed vastly in their views on men, Gloria's gullible approach frequently exasperating Naomi.

'Bully for him, then,' said Naomi grudgingly. She was still smarting over the way Luke had hounded her about the wretched Sister's post, and had then capped it by accusing her of clock-watching.

'You know what your trouble is?' Naomi raised her eyes heavenwards, knowing Gloria was determined to tell her whether she wanted to know or not. 'You're stubborn.'

'I am not! I . . .'

'*Stubborn*,' repeated Gloria with emphasis. 'You made up your mind not to like him, the moment he mentioned that Sister's job.'

'Yes, why *don't* you apply?' asked Richard suddenly, looking hard at Naomi. 'You'd make a damned good one.'

'Oh, for goodness' sake, not you too!' Naomi slammed down her coffee cup angrily, and the cup rattled around in the saucer precariously. 'Why can't people leave me alone!'

'Sorry,' said Richard, backing away looking surprised at the vehemence of her tone. 'It's just that . . .'

'It's just that everyone seems determined to organise my life for me. Well, I've got news for you all—I prefer to organise it myself!' Flinging open the door, Naomi left the coffee room with one abrupt stride, only to ricochet straight off the very solid form of Luke, who happened to be passing, accompanied by Sister Murphy.

'Ah, there you are.' Sister's eyes gleamed with relief at the sight of Naomi. 'A difficult patient has come into Casualty, and I believe Student Nurse Willow is having a few problems. Everyone else seems to have disappeared.'

'I'll bleep Dr Nicholas,' said Naomi hastily, wondering why on earth Patti Willow hadn't rung the rest room. She knew that they had nipped in to snatch a coffee.

'Huh, I hope that young man isn't skiving,' growled the deep voice she had decided she now disliked intensely.

'Dr Nicholas *never* skives!' The words were out before Naomi could stop them.

'As I mentioned before, your concern for Dr Nicholas is touching. Pity it doesn't extend to the Accident and Emergency department.'

Shooting him what she hoped was a suitably venomous glance, but which she noticed crossly appeared to have about as much effect as a ping-pong ball hitting an elephant, Naomi walked ahead. She wished yet again that she could think of a suitably witty and crushing reply, but not a single word of inspiration came. She turned swiftly on her heel away from him. There was nothing she could do except get to Nurse Willow as soon as possible, and call Richard before he was caught drinking coffee.

After calling Richard from a phone out of sight of Luke and Rose Murphy, she made her way to the cubicle, where patient and nurse were obviously having some sort of tussle, judging by the scuffling noises. The reason became obvious as soon as she drew back the cubicle curtain. Patti Willow was wrestling with a young man. He was thin, pale and very scruffy, and one glance was enough to convince Naomi they were almost certainly dealing with a drug addict.

'Why on earth didn't you ring for help before trying to tackle this one on your own?' she grunted, as together she and Patti tried to heave the half-conscious but very aggressive patient up from the floor.

'There wasn't time,' gasped Patti, 'He pushed past Paula on Reception, she didn't even get a chance to fill in an admission form. He just turned up here, and Sister Murphy told me to put him in a cubicle and then call for help. But I haven't been able to leave him to get to a phone.'

Silently Naomi cursed Sister Murphy. Sometimes she really was the limit—talk about bad practice! She must have seen what a difficult customer this one was going to be, but instead of helping, she had left the defenceless student to cope on her own. They certainly did need another Sister in A and E, just to give Rose Murphy a few pointers in correct procedures. Sometimes it seemed that she had forgotten everything she had ever been taught in training. Naomi had no patience with such laxness.

'If we're going to help you, sir,' she said firmly to the patient, 'you'll have to help yourself a little and get up on the couch.'

Her reward was a fist in her face, which luckily did little damage, and a mouthful of obscenities, followed by the same words repeated over and over again. 'I need a fix, damn you, I need a fix!'

Naomi gritted her teeth and tried to look encouragingly at the petrified Patti Willow. 'He'll get his fix,' she said in a low voice, 'but it may not be the one he's wanting.'

The cubicle curtains parted, and Richard Nicholas joined them. 'Where's Sam?' he asked, skirting around the thrashing patient, who by now was more or less on the couch.

'In theatre with a Colles' fracture,' said Naomi. 'Do you want Patti to get Luke Roderick?'

'No, I'll take a history first, then a blood sample, and send it down to the lab so that we can get some idea of what the fellow's been taking. I'll call him after that.'

'OK.' Although Naomi doubted Richard's wisdom in the course of action he'd chosen she said nothing. The patient seemed to have quietened down a little in Richard's presence, and did as he asked. She waited while Richard carefully filled in a history on the admission card. He was not an addict, or so he maintained. Naomi's eyes met Richard's across the patient in a grim smile. In spite of his previous aggressiveness, she felt sorry for the pathetic young man. Who did he think he was kidding, she thought sadly—did he think the needle marks on his arms were invisible? Richard tactfully made no comment, merely saying quietly, 'We'll need a blood sample. Will you sign the consent form here?'

'Sure.' The patient stabbed with the pen at the paper Naomi held out to him. He was beginning to shiver violently, but he just managed to sign his name.

'Right,' said Richard, 'we'll take the blood now.'

Naomi rolled the sleeve well up on the patient's right arm. 'I'll hold his arm steady,' she said to Patti. 'You stay over there.' She didn't say stay well away from the needle, she didn't have to.

'But you . . .' began Patti, knowing very well that blood from a drug addict could be contaminated with one or more serious diseases.

'Don't worry, I'm more experienced than you. I can keep out of the way.'

But even as Naomi spoke, while Richard slid the needle into the vein and started withdrawing the blood sample, the young man suddenly began to vomit uncontrollably, throwing his body from side to side in agony. The needle slipped, and before Richard could prevent it, the flailing arms of the patient caught the syringe, plunging the needle straight into Naomi's unprotected arm.

A horrified second's silence followed, as Richard, Patti and Naomi stared at each other—a silence broken only by the retching of the boy on the couch. All his aggression had dissipated now, and he had disintegrated into cowering, whimpering wretch.

'Oh, my God! whispered Richard. 'What have I done?'

'You didn't do anything,' said Naomi quickly, trying to sound matter-of-fact, even though her heart was racing in her chest, as she ran through the catalogue of diseases she could develop. Possibly hepatitis, and at the worst AIDS.

The cubicle curtains parted abruptly and the tall figure of Luke entered. 'Oh, sir,' Patti blurted out before Naomi could catch her eye and stop her, 'the needle slipped, and went into Naomi!' Her voice trembled, and her wide frightened eyes filled with tears.

At her words, Luke's head jerked up sharply, and his eyes took in the scene. It was very obvious by now, to any informed observer, that the patient was a drug addict. He was thrashing wildly on the couch, moaning and shivering with rigor. Luke looked at Naomi and Richard's pale and worried faces. 'A contaminated needle?' he asked quietly.

'Yes,' said Richard, 'it . . .'

'It was nobody's fault,' interceded Naomi swiftly. 'We were taking blood from the patient. Richard was taking the blood, and the patient moved unexpectedly, knocking the needle into me.'

'Right,' Luke's voice was clipped and precise, 'let's get a fresh sample from the patient. Richard, send it to the lab and write a request card asking for it to be tested for everything—do you understand? Everything!'

'Yes,' muttered Richard miserably, only too well aware of the implications.

'I'll talk to you later,' Luke told Naomi. 'Now, you two,' he nodded at the two girls, 'get out of here before any more accidents happen. I'll help with this chap.' He inclined his head towards the patient, then looked at Richard. 'Take the blood,' he ordered.

A shocked and silent Patti followed Naomi. Once outside, Naomi leaned against the desk in the bay opposite the cubicles, and tried to keep calm. She felt hot and shaky, and however hard she tried to put all the frightening possibilities out of her mind, one thought hammered through her brain. Suppose the patient had AIDS, she would almost certainly catch it, and then what? Suppose she should die? What would happen to Toby? He'd have no one. Aunt Flo wouldn't live for ever, there'd be no one to look after him. He'd have to go into a home for orphans. In spite of her determination to keep calm, she felt hot tears begin to prick behind her eyelids.

Gloria and Sam suddenly appeared, and Patti lost no time in telling them what had happened. Their consternation at the news did little to reassure Naomi, only making her feel more depressed as every moment passed. She needed comforting reassurance from her friends, not horrified gasps.

With a grim single-mindedness she studied her feet, as if her shiny black shoes were the most interesting things she'd ever seen. Intent on blinking back the threatening tears, and trying not to panic, she was unaware that Luke had come to her side, until he firmly grasped her slim wrist in his large hand.

'Come with me,' he said, leading her towards his office.

'But what about the patient?' she nodded towards the cubicle from which a moaning sound still emitted.

'He's quiet for the moment. Sam will stay with him until the ambulance arrives from the Drug Dependence Unit. I've referred him to them, they're the best people to deal with a case like this, we haven't the facilities here.'

'He just barged in, you know, it wasn't . . .'

'Anyone's fault—yes, I know that.' To Naomi's amazement he had all the facts at his fingertips, there was no need for her to explain anything. 'Now, young woman,' he said, pushing her gently inside his office and shutting the door firmly behind him.

'I . . . I know I'll just have to wait until the results of the blood test are back,' said Naomi, adding grimly, 'And there's no need to spell it out for me, I'm well aware of all the possibilities.'

Suddenly two warm, strong hands grasped her shoulders, and she found herself being pulled tenderly towards him. 'I didn't bring you in here to put the fear of God into you, I brought you in to give you some words of comfort.'

'Comfort?' The golden eyes Naomi raised to his were clouded with worry. 'How can you say that? I'm not a fool, you know.'

'Nor a pessimist, I hope.' Hastily Naomi turned her head aside, afraid that all the doubts and fears would overwhelm her; but with a swift movement he caught her chin and forced her face forward and upward. She had no alternative but to look at him, and found herself gazing into eyes as dark, deep and mysterious as the Atlantic Ocean. A strange sensation swept through her, impossible to explain or define even to herself. All she knew was that she felt a kind of solace as she gazed into his eyes. 'He may not have hepatitis or the AIDS virus,' he said firmly.

'But . . .'

'I know, I know—he's a junkie. But he hasn't been mainlining for long, that much I know from what he was able to tell me, and also from the physical examination I made. With luck he's been using clean needles. He's a university student reading biology, so he's had access to a plentiful supply of needles, and he isn't a homosexual.'

'Then there is hope,' breathed Naomi.

'Of course there's hope,' came the rough rejoinder. 'There's always hope, even if our worst fears are realised.'

'I suppose so.' Suddenly Naomi was assailed by doubts and fears again.

'Look, I know it's difficult, but try not to think about it. The moment the blood tests are back, I'll let you know, in the meantime we'll take a sample of your blood as a baseline, just to be on the safe side.'

Gently Luke led Naomi over to a chair, and removed a syringe from the sterile pack. Obediently she stretched out her arm, awaiting the prick of the needle. When he'd finished she silently took the gauze pad from him, and applied it over the needle entry site.

Luke packed and labelled the sample ready for the laboratory, then turned back to Naomi. 'Do you have a family?' he asked suddenly.

She nodded, a clear picture of scruffy little Toby and homely Aunt Flo flashed vividly before her mind.

'Perhaps it would be best not to tell them of this incident. No point in worrying anyone needlessly. All the results will be back by this time tomorrow.'

'Don't worry,' said Naomi, 'I've no intention of telling anyone. The fewer people who know the better.'

He raised his eyebrows at her remark. 'That's a tall order for a hospital, isn't it? Unless things have changed radically since I last worked in a hospital, everyone down to the boiler room attendant will know by tomorrow!' Naomi couldn't help smiling ruefully, knowing very well that this was true. 'That's better,' he said approvingly. 'At least I've coaxed a smile out of you.'

Naomi smiled again. 'Sorry if I overreacted, but it was a bit of a shock.'

'Nonsense, you didn't overreact at all. I've seen grown men go to pieces at a similar incident. You kept your head very well.'

'For a woman, you mean,' Naomi couldn't resist saying drily, some of her common sense and good humour slowly surfacing.

'Hell, no, that's not . . .' He stopped and looked long and hard at her, then suddenly reached over and softly ran one long brown forefinger down the side of her cheek. 'You think it wrong for me to think of women as the gentler sex?'

'Women are people,' said Naomi quickly, wishing she wasn't quite so acutely aware of the touch of his hand, and terrified she'd start blushing, 'just the same as men.'

'Just the same? Good heavens, don't tell me I missed something vital in my anatomy classes!'

'Well . . . you know what I mean,' stammered Naomi, wishing she'd kept her mouth shut, and that he'd take his hand away from her face. Her mind was becoming increasingly confused; even though she tried to tell herself it was ridiculous she found it more and more impossible to think straight.

'I think I know what you mean,' he laughed

softly, 'but I'm not sure that I agree with you.'

Suddenly the long brown fingers stopped caressing her cheek, his hand sliding round to the nape of her neck, gently moving up beneath the silky mass of her neatly pinned chignon. For a moment Naomi could have sworn her heart stopped beating, as slowly, without appearing to exert any effort, he pulled her towards him. Or was it that he stepped forward to her? She couldn't be sure. All she knew was that he was much too close, much too close indeed.

That was her last coherent thought before his tanned face blotted out the light, as he bent his head to kiss her full on the mouth.

Naomi had been kissed plenty of times before, but nothing had prepared her for the bone-melting, knee-weakening effect of Luke's kiss. It must be because he's so well practised, she thought hazily, knowing she ought to resist for her own sake, but not wanting to, trapped as she was by the rising tide of elation pulsing through her veins.

At last he drew back slowly, and gazed down at her. Naomi kept her fluttering lashes downcast, knowing she daren't look into those dark green eyes, because if she did she'd drown. Instead she muttered the first words that came into her head. 'You shouldn't have done that, you might catch AIDS.'

'Rubbish, you can't pass on HIV through kissing, and even if it was possible, it's a risk I'm willing to take.' His voice was husky as he bent his head towards her trembling mouth once more.

But this time common sense prevailed, and Naomi extricated herself from his arms and made a beeline for the door. 'Thanks for the goodwill gesture,' she said, purposely instilling a casual note into her voice. 'You've successfully restored my sense of equilibrium.'

'Oh, is *that* all?' She averted her eyes hastily from the wickedly suggestive gleam in his eyes. 'I usually achieve a greater degree of success than that!'

'Oh well, you can't win them all,' retorted Naomi lightly, but at the same time she felt slightly irritated. It was annoying to think that he must know how earth-shattering his kisses were. It will do him good to know they don't work every time, she tried to tell herself, wishing it was the truth, and that it hadn't worked for her either!

'So it seems,' came the low chuckle as she left the office. 'But at least I'm certain it's taken your mind off your immediate problems.'

Suddenly Naomi felt strangely deflated. He'd kissed her just to shock her back to normality, to make her forget, momentarily at least, that she might have caught something disastrous. Unfortunately, his shock tactics had succeeded far better than he knew!

For the rest of the afternoon Naomi had difficulty in concentrating. The others all put it down to the fact that she'd had a terrible shock, and waiting for the blood test results was like having the sword of Damocles suspended by a hair over her head.

'I'm not surprised, I'd be at my wits' end too,' whispered Gloria sympathetically, retrieving the second patient Naomi had sent to X-Ray by mistake, when they should have gone to the plaster room.

Naomi gave a wan smile. She felt a fraud. Of course she was worried about the blood test, but somehow the effect of Luke's kiss was even more worrying. I've got my priorities all wrong, she thought, feeling hopelessly muddled. I ought to be worrying about the accident, not Luke Roderick! I've always been immune to men like him, men that are too smooth, too self-assured. She tried to blot out the memory of that intoxicating kiss, telling herself that he was like one of the oily Latin lovers in Sister Murphy's books. But then she rejected that idea—no, that was being *too* cruel. Luke Roderick couldn't possibly, by any stretch of the imagination, be described as oily!

The thing you've got to remember, my girl, she told herself walking back that evening to her bed-sit, is that he was using his training in psychology! That's all it was, and it doesn't mean a thing, other than that he's thoroughly professional and ruthless. Determined not to let one of his nurses go to pieces, and make the unit short-handed, he'd used the nearest means at his disposal! And it had worked.

All the same, she couldn't help wishing morosely that he'd used some other form of psychology, one that wouldn't prove so hard to forget.

CHAPTER FOUR

THE WATER'S EDGE was exceptionally busy for a Monday night. A party of American businessmen were being entertained by a local shipbuilding firm, and Naomi was rushed off her feet attending to their every need. Every drink had to be 'on the rocks' and the kitchen staff were going frantic as they rapidly began to run out of ice.

'Stall them, will you,' the manager ordered Naomi, 'while Dick rustles up some more ice.'

Stalling proved easier said than done, but at least it gave Naomi plenty to think about. And it wasn't until the end of her shift, when she and Molly, the lady who did the washing up, were finishing the dregs of a bottle of Chablis between them that Naomi found she even had time to give the events of the afternoon a thought.

Twirling the wine, watching the slaty green liquid glisten through the points of light on the finely cut crystal glass, she smiled to herself. Hard work was a good salve for problems, she reflected. Her evening job had proved to be a boon, that particular day, in more ways than one.

'A penny for them,' said Molly curiously, watching the changing expressions chase one another across Naomi's expressive face.

Nobody at the Water's Edge knew that Naomi was a nurse during the day, because she purposely kept the two parts of her life separate, always afraid that someone from the nursing hierarchy would find out she was doing what was strictly forbidden—namely moonlighting, although she had told Molly that she lived at Longstone with Toby and Aunt Flo at weekends, and Molly always wanted to hear about Toby's latest escapades. She was a comfortable, unassuming middle-aged woman, with no children of her own, and she took pleasure in hearing about Toby; always knitting him woolly hats and mittens for the winters. Naomi could never bring herself to tell her that Toby refused to wear them, except for the occasions when she took a photograph of him with them on, especially to show Molly.

Molly's query coming out of the blue startled her. She shrugged and said lightly, 'My thoughts aren't worth even a penny, Molly. The only thing I'm thinking about is the fact that my feet hurt!'

'I'm not surprised,' retorted Molly severely, pushing her own feet forward. They were sensibly clad is soft leather shoes which allowed them to spread happily in all directions, giving plenty of room for her bunions. 'You should wear shoes like I've got,' she added.

Naomi laughed. 'Perhaps I will,' she said, privately thinking she'd have to be six feet under before anyone would get shoes like Molly's on her feet! Draining her wine glass, she stood up. 'I must go now,' she said firmly, discouraging further questions. She didn't want to hurt Molly's feelings, but didn't feel like talking. Tired, and feeling vulnerable, she knew it would be all to easy to inadvertently say more than she intended.

Now that the evening's rush was over, the incidents of the afternoon loomed once more, beginning to intrude uncomfortably into her mind. The sooner she got to bed, the better. A good night's sleep was what she needed before duty began at eight-thirty the next morning. It was already one-thirty, and to say that she felt tired would be the understatement of the day.

A good night's sleep, however, was something nature decided to deny her. Usually after her bath, she fell into bed, and the sleep of exhaustion engulfed her the moment her head hit the pillow. But tonight she couldn't sleep. The results of the blood test hovered over her menacingly, but almost equally disturbing was the face of Luke Roderick. It seemed as if her memory had caught a glimpse of his dark, tanned face, with the deep laughter lines either side of his mouth, and imprinted it indelibly on her mind. It was the split second before he had kissed her, and try as she might to erase all thoughts of him, every time she closed her eyes he was there bending over her. In her imagination she could almost feel the touch of his warm lips on her eager mouth.

Eventually, in sheer desperation, after rummaging around in her dressing table drawers she found some sleeping pills, and swallowed half of one. Richard had given them to her several months before, when she had ricked her ankle badly and couldn't sleep because of the pain. She'd never resorted to taking them then, but now, she reasoned, was an emergency.

The consequence was disastrous. When her morning alarm shrilled, and she attempted to leap up in her usual fashion, she found she couldn't. Eventually she managed to struggle out of bed, feeling like death warmed up.

'Oh hell!' she groaned in horror, looking at her puffy eyes and pallid face in the bathroom mirror. 'They really will think I'm going down with some dreaded disease!' The bright-eyed, suntanned girl of yesterday had disappeared, and in her place was a distinctly seedy-looking creature, who felt as awful as she looked.

Jamming ice cubes against her eyes and drinking black coffee at the same time, was a difficult procedure, but Naomi managed it somehow. She managed to reduce some of the puffiness around her eyes, but her cheeks retained a stubbornly unhealthy pallor. Hastily sloshing on vast amounts of blusher and eye make-up, as an attempted remedy, she then decided it made her look as if she was about to audition for the part of a clown, and scrubbed it all off again. The upshot was that she arrived at A and E looking as pale as when she'd awoked, and wishing she could spend another five hours in bed.

'You look awful!' Gloria and Richard shrieked together as soon as they saw her.

'Thanks a bundle. Anyway, it's all your fault.'

Naomi glowered at Richard through eyelids which felt as if they ought to be held up with pit-props. 'I couldn't sleep last night, so I took half of one of those damned pills you gave me.'

'But they're not supposed to be long-acting,' said Richard with a frown. 'What time did you take it?'

'Four o'clock this morning,' said Naomi wearily. 'I told you I couldn't sleep, by that time I was desperate.'

'Then by rights you should still be asleep now,' said Richard. 'I suppose you got up at seven as usual.'

Naomi nodded, realising as Richard spoke that she'd been stupid to take the pill so late. But at the time anything had seemed worth trying, just to escape the image of the man now stalking down the corridor towards them.

'I'd better collect the first patient for this shift,' she muttered, beating a hasty retreat. 'Ready, Richard?'

Richard and Gloria took their cues from her expression, rightly guessing that their new boss was advancing upon them. Gloria shot off in the direction of the referral clinic, where she was due to work with Dr Sengupta, their part-time casualty officer, and Richard busied himself with some X-rays from the night before.

The morning started with a trickle of minor injuries, and gradually Naomi began to feel better, as the effect of the sleeping tablet wore off. A large cup of coffee and a plentiful supply of sweet biscuits, which Richard insisted she have at ten-thirty, did the trick. She felt back to normal, although she still looked rather pale and fragile.

'I can't understand it,' said Richard, looking at her as she handed him the notes of the next patient he was about to see. 'You looked so well yesterday. You're not worrying yourself to death, are you?'

Naomi smiled at him reassuringly. 'No, I'm not,' she said. It was true—apart from some minor twinges of worry, she hadn't thought too much about the impending blood results. She knew why she looked pale—the evening's work at the Water's Edge, plus the effect of the sleeping pill, was enough to make even the most intrepid person look peaky. 'You know me,' she joked, 'I only look healthy at the weekends! The rest of the week I'm pale and interesting. Now, see what you can do for this patient with a bee sting, I'm sure you'll find the case interesting!'

Richard raised his eyebrows. 'Bee sting?' he queried, sounding suspicious. 'Not on the throat, is it?'

'No,' replied Naomi, trying to keep a straight face, 'on the breast.'

'Well, really! Fancy coming to Casualty for a thing . . .' The words died in his throat as he twitched back the cubicle curtains to behold a ravishing blonde, minus a blouse, but clad in a pink pinafore suit which did very little to conceal her extremely well-endowed bosom.

Naomi bit her lip with amusement and stood well behind him, as he suddenly switched on his most helpful 'I am a doctor, now what can I do for you' voice.

Tossing back her silvery mane of peroxide blonde hair, the girl smiled, exposing a set of perfectly even white teeth. Every one of them capped, I bet, thought Naomi, trying not to feel envious.

'Oh, hello, Doctor. I'm a model.' The girl spoke with a prounounced Birmingham accent which seemed incongruous with her *Dynasty*-type appearance. 'A nude model, and I'm due to do a photographic session today, but I've just been stung . . . here.' She slipped a pink strap off one suntanned shoulder and patted one equally tanned and well rounded breast in a worried fashion.

The problem was plain enough to see. Uncerneath the nipple was a bright red swelling; it looked like another nipple. 'I see . . . er . . . yes,' said Richard, gulping.

Naomi stifled a smile with difficulty at his expression. He must have seen plenty of bosoms in his medical life, but this one obviously affected him differently!

'They only like one nipple on nudes,' said the girl with an engagingly honest smile. 'You know, one on each side!' She grinned at Naomi. 'You know, it's a real drag,' she confessed, 'having to keep your body perfect all the time. I'm looking forward to the day when I've made enough money to let myself go to seed.'

Naomi laughed. 'I think that would be a pity,' she said truthfully. 'Most girls would give their eye teeth to look the way you do.'

Richard moved forward cautiously. 'I'll have to examine you,' he said, 'before I decide on a course of action.'

'Prod away,' said the girl, whose name Naomi knew from the notes to be Melanie, and without embarrassment exposed the other perfectly formed breast for comparison.

After a moment's hesitation, Richard started a physical examination, but on placing his hands on her chest almost immediately turned away and holted out of the cubicle. 'I think I need a second opinion,' he muttered as he fled.

Melanie was busily telling Naomi how she's always wanted to be a nurse, but couldn't manage to get any O-levels, when Richard came hurrying back, accompanied by Luke. 'If you could just feel the breast, sir,' he said in a low voice, 'the swelling seems to have spread through the entire mass of tissue.'

Naomi told herself it was completely irrational even to think of such a thing, but the fact that Luke seemed entirely unmoved by the perfect bosom spread out, in all its glory, before him, gladdened her heart. Of course jealousy wasn't a word she would have admitted, not even to her subconscious! but she couldn't help thinking that Melanie's perfect bust was enough to give any girl an inferiority complex.

With swift, deft movements Luke examined both breasts, then looked at the glamorous patient and raised his eyebrows. 'Oh yes, Doctor, they're both silicone,' said Melanie in answer to his unspoken question. 'I was as flat as Nurse there before I had this job done.'

She patted the jutting objects in question proudly, and Naomi felt herself blushing a brilliant scarlet as both Richard and Luke automatically turned and looked at her when Melanie made the comparison.

Melanie noticed the blush. 'Don't worry about it, dearie,' she said kindly. 'Some men are turned on by flat chests, but I'll give you the name of the doctor in London in case you feel like doing something about them.'

'Thank you,' choked Naomi. She could have cheerfully strangled the two men with their stethoscopes; they were both grinning inanely. Naomi's glower only succeeded in stretching their grins from ear to ear.

Melanie was soon dealt with and sent on her way with an aerosol spray to help take down the swelling, although photography for that day was out of the question. To Naomi's relief she didn't get an opportunity to give her the address she'd promised, as by the time Melanie was ready, Naomi had already left the cubicle in answer to an urgent call, and was busy in the ambulance bay with an emergency which had just arrived without the usual prior warning.

One look at the patient, minus a finger on one hand, but with it carefully wrapped up in a box of ice, decided her. 'Keep him here,' she told the ambulance men. 'I think Mr Roderick may well be sending him on to Modbury.'

She was pretty certain micro-surgery was on the cards. The patient looked in good physical shape, and appeared to be relatively unshocked. She was positive he'd be sent out to Modbury, the nearest micro-surgical unit, and she knew the less time wasted the better.

'Luke, we have a patient for micro-surgery, I think.' It was only afterwards that she realised that she'd used his first name without embarrassment, and without even thinking about it. Luke joined her and together they quickly made their way to the waiting ambulance in the emergency bay. A quick examination, and a brief questioning of the patient and the ambulance men, and Luke made his decision.

'Well done,' he told the two ambulance men. 'Your quick thinking has given this patient the chance of having his finger restored. And with any luck, he'll be as good as new. Take him immediately to Modbury. We'll phone and give them all the details so that he can go straight into surgery.' As he spoke he took a blood sample. 'We'll even be able to give them your blood group,' he said, smiling at the remarkably stoical patient, 'although I doubt you'll need blood, you haven't lost much.'

'Thanks, guv.' The patient, a middle-aged butcher, was taking it all in his stride. 'Thought I'd lose me finger like me dad,' he said calmly. 'One of the hazards of the trade, you know. Bacon slicers can be damned tricky things.'

Luke nodded approvingly at the man's calmness, which Naomi knew could prove to be a life-saver in such situations and gave her the blood sample. 'Tell them to phone us with the type, but not to cross-match,' he said, 'then ring Modbury and give them the lowdown.' He handed her the brief summary he'd scribbled out. 'That should be enough for them to be going on with.'

As he spoke he flashed a smile at her, his dark eyes seeming to lighten with a thousand glinting lights, and his hand brushed against hers. Naomi swallowed hard. Damn the man, why was it he could so easily disconcert her! And it didn't help one little bit when it was so obviously a one-sided effect. She could see that all Luke's concentration was on the matter in hand, which was where her own should have been. She knew he had forgotten about her as he turned back to the patient with a final few words of advice before he was taken off to Modbury.

Naomi obeyed his instructions to the letter, and by the time she had completed all her tasks, it was already time for her lunch break. She made her way down to the canteen to meet Gloria, who was on the same rota as herself. Gloria, as usual, had already arrived. Somehow she always managed to get away on time, unlike Naomi, who was invariably late. But Naomi was glad to see she'd saved a place for her at a table in the middle of the huge and crowded canteen. It was one-thirty, the time most staff and students took their lunch, and there was hardly a spare seat left in the place.

'Hi,' said Gloria through a mouthful of cottage cheese and lettuce. She was on a permanent diet, and envied Naomi who could eat steak pie and chips every day if she chose, and still not put on weight.

Naomi slid down into the chair beside Gloria with her tray, automatically kicking off her tight shoes. 'Hi, and thanks for saving the seat. How were things your side of Cas?'

'Not as exciting as yours,' said Gloria, who'd heard about the silicone implant and the severed finger, 'although I did meet a rather gorgeous man this morning, one of the patients. His name is Gordon, and he's a local solicitor and,' she added, 'we've fixed a date.' She paused a moment, looking at Naomi speculatively. 'I already know his friend,' she said, 'and Gordon has suggested a foursome if I could find someone else, so I suggested you.'

'Me?' Naomi was aghast. There was no way she could go out in the evenings.

'Oh, come on,' said Gloria, 'have a bit of fun for a change.'

Naomi pulled a face. Even if she had been free, a blind date was not her cup of tea. 'I haven't got time,' she protested. 'Anyway, I'm too old for blind dates, that sort of thing is for teenagers. But I'm flattered you asked me,' she added, not wanting to hurt Gloria's feelings.

'Look, I told you I know Gordon's friend,' persisted Gloria. 'He's nice, he would be perfect for you.'

'If you're trying to play matchmaker forget it,' said Naomi abruptly.

'You ought to go out sometimes,' said Gloria earnestly. 'I don't understand you, Naomi, really I don't. You ought to take an interest in men.'

'Men leave me cold,' said Naomi tersely, wishing Gloria would give up. 'I've got more important things to think of.'

'Oh? Such as?' Gloria's eyes widened.

'Is this seat taken? Luke stood beside them, a laden tray in his hands.

The seat beside Naomi was vacant, and she had to admit, after a surreptitious scan around the milling crowd in the canteen, that it did appear to be the only one actually free.

'No, it's free,' she said a trifle reluctantly, at the same time wondering anxiously if he had overheard their conversation. A bald statement such as 'men leave me cold' was hardly in keeping with her unbridled response to his kiss of the day before.

Naomi could see Gloria was pleased Luke had joined them, and suspected she was wondering how much information about his personal life she could prize out of him, in the short time available for social chit-chat. Her next remark confirmed Naomi's suspicions.

'Have you managed to find a house yet?' she asked innocently. 'Most of the consultants live on the west side of the city, towards the Forest area. The schools are so much better out that way.'

Naomi smothered a smile. Gloria's subtle way of finding out whether Luke had marriage and a family in mind was transparently obvious to her.

'That's not a problem I shall have to contend with,' said Luke affably, not seeming to mind Gloria's probing. 'I'm not married, and I'm looking for a house by the sea. Sailing is the love of my life.'

'Oh, you'd love it where Naomi lives,' said Gloria. 'I've never been there, but everyone says . . .' She stopped mid-sentence as Naomi smartly kicked her on the ankle. The last thing she wanted was Luke Roderick living in her neck of the woods. 'Everyone says it's very nice,' finished Gloria lamely, shooting Naomi a puzzled look.

'Oh?' Luke sounded interested. 'Where is that?'

'To the east of the town,' replied Naomi quickly, cursing her friend. 'Not that it's very good for sailing,' she said, lying through her teeth. It was one of the best places for miles around. 'But I believe there's a gorgeous marina and some beautiful new houses being built just along the coast towards Bournemouth.' She mentioned Bournemouth as it was as far from Longstone as she could think of, and it was perfectly true that an expensive new marina was being developed there.

'I must have a look,' said Luke. 'Perhaps if you're free you could show me this weekend.'

'I'm very sorry, but I'm completely tied up,' answered Naomi quickly. His unexpected invitation surprised and unnerved her. Finishing the last mouthful of her lunch, she stood up. 'Please excuse me,' she said formally, 'but I've got to dash. Are you coming, Gloria?'

Gloria hesitated a moment, but then got up and followed her. 'Why did you refuse his invitation?' she hissed as soon as they were out of earshot. 'Luke Roderick asked you out, don't you realise that? You lucky girl!'

'That last thing I want is to spend my off-duty time with Mr Roderick,' answered Naomi, wishing that things had been different and she could have said yes. But there was no point, already she knew she was dangerously attracted to him—no point in laying herself open to hurt. He touched a raw nerve in her emotions, but realistically she acknowledged that to him she was just another fairly attractive woman, one he'd soon lose interest in when he found she had domestic ties. He had already made it clear in reply to Gloria's question that marriage was not on his agenda, so presumably that meant he wasn't over-fond of children.

'Well, really! There's no accounting for taste.' Gloria's astounded voice brought her unhappy wandering thoughts to heel. 'If he'd asked me I should have jumped at the chance.'

She looked so woebegone that Naomi laughed. 'What about this Gordon?' she said. 'I thought you said he was gorgeous.'

'Well, yes, he is.' Gloria cheered up. 'But it would have been nice to have two strings to my bow!'

'Incorrigible, that's what you are,' Naomi reprimanded an unpenitent Gloria.

The two girls collected their coffee and squeezed into the crowded coffee lounge; here there were no seats and they were forced to huddle together in a corner sipping their coffee.

'Although why you're not interested in a man like Luke Roderick I shall never understand,' said Gloria, her thoughts returning to their new consultant. She wrinkled her nose in flagrant disbelief at such a phenomenon.

Naomi sighed. It was impossible to explain, especially as Gloria was one of those open people who just had to tell everyone everything. Whereas Naomi had a secret—Toby and the job at the Water's Edge. If only the nursing hierarchy weren't so difficult about nurses taking second jobs, she wouldn't have had to keep it such a secret. But they were, so her hands were tied. She desperately needed the money, and moonlighting was the only way to get it.

Coffee finished, they were soon back in Casualty, and the afternoon sped by, although they had nothing as dramatic as silcone implants and amputated fingers.

'A very run-of-the-mill afternoon,' grumbled Gloria. 'The only excitement I've had has been a sprained ankle on a driving instructor. Although,' she brightened visibly, 'he did ask if he could see me again.'

'Two men after you in one day!' Naomi teased. 'Perhaps with the last one you could wangle some free driving lessons.' She knew Gloria had been struggling erratically with her driving for months.

'Two minds with but a single thought,' replied Gloria with a wide grin.

Although nothing terribly exciting had been happening, there certainly wasn't much time for gossiping, and the staff of A and E were kept constantly on the run. So when the envelope came down from Haematology addressed to 'Mr Roderick' Naomi was too busy to think anything of it, and detailed Patti Willow to take it in to him.

She had managed successfully to put all thoughts of the previous day's incident into cold storage at the back of her mind, but a few seconds later, when she was summoned to Luke's office, the penny suddenly dropped. It must be the results of the blood test on the drug addict, and all at once the fears came flooding back. It was with a dry mouth and racing heart that she tapped at Luke's door and went in at his bidding.

'Well?' she said, running the tip of her tongue around her lips. They were dry with nerves.

'You're not about to be a martyr for the cause of medicine, and join those names in the hallowed halls of fame,' replied Luke, looking very solemn.

'What exactly does that mean?' Naomi

demanded. She wanted to hear the reply in plan English.

'This,' he said, and getting up handed her the haematology report card.

Naomi took the card and stared at it. At first she couldn't read a thing, the words danced about as if they had individual lives of their own, but then two words leapt out from the card, 'Negative, Negative'.

'Then everything is all right!' she breathed softly, hardly daring to believe her eyes. Then inexplicably her limbs started trembling, and without warning she found herself sobbing in a flood of uncontrollable tears of relief. The fear she had thought she had so successfully banished had been there lurking in the background all the time, and now the dam was breached by the floodgate of relief.

'Women!' erupted Luke in some exasperation. 'Why can't they cry when there's something to cry about? Why do they always cry when it's good news?' He put his arms around her, and Naomi weakly let her body be moulded closely against his hard-muscled form.

'I don't know,' she sobbed, suddenly feeling ecstatically happy and ridiculously feminine and vulnerable as she leaned against him. She was drawn to him like a magnet, his nearness promising a tantalising mixture of fortitude and intoxicating agitation. 'Oh, it's such a relief to know I'm not going to die,' she blurted out between sobs.

'I wouldn't count on that,' came the wry reply. 'At the rate you're going, we shall *both* drown!'

CHAPTER FIVE

IF SISTER MURPHY hadn't chosen that precise moment to barge in, letting out a squawk of amazement at the sight confronting her, Naomi was sure Luke would have kissed her again — if vibes were anything to go by! Surely, she thought, he must feel something! Once in his arms, she longed to feel his lips on hers, every fibre of her being was willing him to kiss her.

All the thoughts of the previous night, when she had battled desperately to drive him out of her mind and forget the kiss of that afternoon, were consigned to oblivion. So too were her words to Gloria of only a few hours previously—*men leave me cold*. Mixed in with the relief at the negative blood results was the sure and certain knowledge that Luke did not leave her in the slightest bit cold. Quite the reverse, in fact!

However, Rose Murphy's very passable imitation of a chicken laying an egg, and the noise of the door as she hastily slammed it shut before any other members of A and E could see the scene in Luke's office, brought Naomi back from the realms of fantasy she'd happily allowed herself to drift into. Luke released her, and she came down to earth with a disagreeably hard jolt.

'I'm sorry,' she muttered, wiping her eyes, glad she hadn't kept on all the mascara she'd applied so heavily that morning. 'I don't know what came over me.'

'That's quite all right,' said Luke, an enigmatic expression she couldn't fathom lurking in the depths of his deep green eyes. 'It was to be expected in the circumstances.'

His mobile mouth curved in a barely perceptible but nevertheless extremely sensual smile, as he passed her a snowy white, crisp handkerchief, Naomi's own small whisper of cotton proving inadequate for the job.

Silently Naomi took the proffered handkerchief and wiped her eyes and blew her nose. Watching him as he turned to speak to Sister Murphy, she suddenly had the most disconcerting feeling that he had known precisely what she'd been thinking when she'd been in his arms. And that he knew he had only had to lift his little finger and open his arms to her, and she'd fall straight into them again without a moment's hesitation!

'The blood results came,' he said in answer to Sister's wide-eyed stare.

'Oh, my goodness!' A tragic expression settled over her face and Rose Murphy lowered her ample girth heavily into the chair beside the door. 'I'm so sorry,' she said slowly.

Naomi gulped, something halfway between a laugh and a hiccup, as she realised poor Sister Murphy thought the results were positive. 'It's all right, Sister,' she said, wiping her still wet eyes again, 'the results are negative.'

'Then why . . .?'

'I don't know. Ridiculous, isn't it?' said Naomi with a faint smile. 'I was so relieved that I just burst into tears. I'm afraid I thoroughly disgraced myself.'

'A good strong cup of tea is what you need.' Sister Murphy's officiousness reasserted itself. The enormous dark blue uniform rose majestically, and a fat arm leaned heavily on Naomi's shoulders. At the same time Naomi found herself drawn purposefully towards the door. 'We'll go and leave poor Luke in peace.'

'I'm sorry,' said Naomi to Luke, having now regained most of her composure, 'it won't happen again.'

'Don't worry about it. Any time!' came the quiet reply, too quiet for Sister Murphy to hear as she was already talking, calling out to Student Nurse Willow, telling her to put the kettle on.

Naomi was very glad Sister hadn't heard his remark, and even more glad that she had missed the extremely broad and wicked wink Luke had given her as they left his office. I really will have to be very careful, she told herself sternly, the wretched man obviously thinks I'm putty in his hands. Suddenly she felt herself blushing as an irreverent thought flew into her head. How nice it would be to let herself be that piece of putty!

For the rest of that week Naomi was very careful to keep what she considered to be as safe a distance as possible between herself and Luke Roderick.

There were plenty of nurses swooning about the TV star of Accident and Emergency. Sinbad the Surgeon had become quite a celebrity throughout the hospital. There was no need for her to become another one of his camp followers, Naomi told herself firmly.

Luckily her rota had been changed, and two clinics she was due to have done with Luke were given to Gloria, while she had been given the task of coping with the daily grind of Casualty. Sister Murphy had explained it by saying that as Richard Nicholas was away on study leave, she felt the new locum could do with more experienced help; but Naomi had a shrewd suspicion that it had something to do with her being found clasped to Luke Roderick's manly chest! Although whether Sister was trying to protect her, or whether perhaps she didn't approve of her staff nurses being found in the arms of the senior surgeon, Naomi didn't know. Whatever the reason, it suited her fine.

Friday afternoon arrived and Naomi began to look forward to the weekend. Only a few more hours and she'd be at home again, with her beloved Toby and Aunt Flo. She glanced at her watch and sighed. The time always seemed to go so slowly on Friday afternoons.

It was about halfway through the afternoon when Timmy Galbraith was brought in by his mother. 'Painful feet' was what Paula the receptionist had written as cause for admission to Casualty. Naomi raised her eyebrows at the rather strange note, and went into the cubicle to take the necessary case history, before calling Dr Rogers, their locum senior house officer.

Timmy's mother was a glamorous university lecturer, a Doctor of Psychology. She was divorced, and Timmy, one of her two children, lived with her, the other with her ex-husband. Timmy was as scruffy as his mother was glamorous, and it didn't take Naomi long to assess that not only was he unwashed and unkempt, but that he was unloved, his mother considering him to be an obstacle in the way of her career.

'How long has he had this problem?' she asked, looking at Timmy's grubby feet, the soles of which were covered in huge and obviously very painful verrucas.

To grow as large as they had must have taken some time, and he would have been in pain for all of that time. But Dr Galbraith merely answered irritably, 'How on earth should I know? I only noticed him hobbling today when I went to buy him new shoes. He's never complained before. Mrs Oliver, my daily, usually looks after him, I have very little time to spare.'

That's quite obvious, thought Naomi sadly. Her heart went out to Timmy, who was the same age as Toby, but whereas Toby was a confident eight-year-old, boisterous and full of fun, Timmy was cowed and worried-looking. His big eyes, staring at her from behind large cheap-rimmed glasses, were brimming with tears.

'Don't worry,' she said softly, 'you've got verrucas, that's a sort of wart. We'll soon be able to make them better, and then your feet won't hurt at all.'

'I've never been in hospital,' his reedy little voice piped up.

'There's nothing to worry about.' Naomi smiled and patted his hand, then stood up. 'I'll get the doctor to look at you and decide on the best course of action.'

'About time too,' snapped Dr Galbraith, looking at her watch. 'I've got a dinner appointment in London this evening, and Timmy has to be dropped off at Mrs Oliver's first.'

Unpleasant, self-centred woman! fumed Naomi as she walked away. If she had looked after her son properly, his feet would never have got into such a dreadful state. Without further ado she hurried into the office-cum-coffee room where she expected to find Dr Rogers. However, there was no sign of Patrick Rogers, only Luke. He raised his eyebrows at her hurried entrance.

'Problems?'

'A case in Casualty. I was looking for Patrick Rogers.'

He levered his long form up from the low armchair, and stood up. 'I've sent him round to X-Ray. I'll come—what is it?'

'Verrucas,' said Naomi.

'Verrucas!' Luke stopped, and placed a restraining hand on her arm. 'We're running a casualty department, not a foot clinic!'

'You wait until you see them,' replied Naomi, 'and the poor kid who has them.' She moved her arm away from his hand, and started walking quickly back towards the cubicle area, wishing her pulse wouldn't erupt like Vesuvius at his touch.

Luke threw her a curious glance and followed her towards the curtained cubicle. Once inside, however, Naomi was very glad it was Luke who was there, and not Patrick Rogers. For one thing, he worked his magic way with the child, and for another he very quickly and successfully put the overbearing Dr Galbraith in her place. Without being rude, he managed to let her know in no uncertain terms just what he thought of the standard of care of her son. A telephone call later and he had arranged for Timmy to be admitted to the paediatric ward for a few days.

'But merely for warts?' his mother said in a disbelieving voice. 'That's what your nurse said they were—only warts.'

'A form of wart, yes,' said Luke, his tone scathing, 'which normally can be dealt with on an outpatient basis with no problem at all. But verrucas as bad as this are extremely painful, and I'd be failing in my duty as a doctor to let him try to walk out of here before we've been able to give him some treatment. The paediatricians are quite happy to take him as they have some empty beds. So we'll have him in and get the treatment started.'

Timmy went off quite happily with Linda, the plump staff nurse from Paeds, not giving a backward glance at his mother, who went rushing off to collect night clothes, toothbrush and other toiletries.

'It will give him a boost to be the centre of attention for a few days,' said Luke, watching the thin figure hobbling beside Linda. 'It's not much, but at least it's better than nothing.'

'Yes,' said Naomi softly, 'poor unloved Timmy.'

'A typical case of a one-parent family,' snorted Luke. 'It's always the same—not enough attention, not enough time, and not enough love.'

'That's not true! It's not always like that,' cried Naomi, thinking of Toby, who in a way was in a one-parent situation, but who had plenty of love. 'Some one-parent families are very successful.'

'I've yet to see one,' said Luke disdainfully. 'The ending of marriage contractual obligations usually means the abdication of custodial obligations as well.'

'I don't know about marriage, but I'm sure you're wrong about the one-parent issue,' said Naomi positively, warming to the subject. 'One or two parents, or even only an aunt, that isn't important. It's love that matters.'

'What are you getting so hot under the collar for?' said Luke, looking at her quizzically. 'As a spinster you've hardly got first-hand knowledge.'

Naomi felt herself flushing guiltily. 'As a bachelor I suppose you have,' she snapped, annoyed at his arbitrary judgement.

'I've probably seen more cases of child neglect than you . . .'

'Oh yes, no doubt while you were gallivanting round the world pretending you were Sinbad the

Sailor!'

'There's no need to take that attitude,' began Luke, clearly puzzled by Naomi's belligerent tone of voice.

'I shall take whatever attitude I see fit,' said Naomi curtly, her bad temper due in part to the sudden rush of guilt he'd provoked—the niggling thought, always lurking uneasily at the back of her mind, the fact that she'd never bothered, or wanted to find Toby's father. She looked at the watch swinging from her pocket, and the guilty feeling increased. The nurses' watch had been the last thing Tiffany had given her before she died. 'It's four-thirty, time I was off duty,' she said abruptly, and without a further word hurried away in the direction of the nurses' changing room.

Luke remained standing where he was, one hand thoughtfully stroking his chin as he watched her agitated figure disappear down the corridor.

Timmy's thin little face, and Luke's harsh words of judgement on one-parent families, continued to haunt Naomi all the way back to Longstone that evening. Even the brilliance of the sky, slashed across with pinks and oranges, reflected back from the mirror-smooth sea, failed to raise her spirits, or dispel her uneasy conscience.

It wasn't until Toby and Stubbs came rushing along the dusty lane to greet her that her doubts and fears disappeared. Toby might be an orphan, but he couldn't be loved more, and one look at him told her that he thrived on it. But he wouldn't be like this if it wasn't for Aunt Flo, the niggling little voice reminded her. Perhaps even Timmy would have had a different life if his mother had had someone to help her share the responsibility. But that wouldn't change the fact that Dr Galbraith was a career woman and didn't love Timmy, whereas at heart Naomi was a home-lover, and loved Toby passionately. If life had turned out differently she would have loved children of her own. But her role in life was different; she was mother and aunt rolled into one.

As she hugged his wriggling, warm little body close to her, Naomi wondered yet again if she'd done the right thing all those years ago in not seeking out Dirk Roderigues. But she brushed the thought away. It was too late now, he had probably forgotten that Tiffany had ever existed. She smiled wryly. Now he was a millionaire, and very famous, she could imagine his reaction if she tried to rake up something from the past, something that included the responsibility of a small boy. As usual her mind went round and round in circles, and she ended up as uncertain as ever.

She was almost tempted to mention her fresh doubts to Aunt Flo that night, as they sat outside in the garden. It was a balmy evening and Toby had long ago fallen asleep in his room upstairs, the faithful Stubbs, ever vigilant, snoring loudly at the foot of the bed. The words wouldn't come, though, something held them back. Aunt Flo had once said let sleeping dogs lie, and that was precisely what they had done. It would only upset

Toby to stir things up now.

If Aunt Flo thought Naomi quieter than usual, she kept her own counsel, merely reminding her that she'd promised to take Toby sailing on Sunday with Bob and Janet.

Naomi groaned—she had forgotten. Sailing was her least favourite occupation, she always felt nauseous, even on the calmest day. So when Sunday morning dawned with a stiff breeze and puffy white clouds scudding for all they were worth across the sky, she tentatively mentioned at breakfast that perhaps bad weather was blowing up and they wouldn't be able to go.

Bob and Janet, however, had other ideas. They were fanatical sailors, and lived in a converted fisherman's cottage in Longstone harbour. The sea wall formed part of their garden wall, and they moored their boat, a nineteen-foot Hunter, right outside the cottage.

'Too windy? Rubbish!' said Janet heartily, when Naomi mentioned her doubts. 'A good force six on the Beaufort scale is just what we need to get us across to the Island in record time.'

'Yes!' shouted Toby, bobbing up and down excitedly. He looked like an animated Action Man, kitted out in his yellow sea-boots and brilliant orange lifejacket; all of which he had worn from the moment he'd taken his pygamas off that morning. 'Look at the white horses, Naomi!'

Naomi did look, and her heart sank. Her stomach seethed alarmingly at the mere sight. Outside the shelter of the little harbour, large waves tossed their foaming crests, as if daring them to venture out, and the spray blew inland, salting her nervous lips.

It was the first Sunday in August and they'd planned to sail over to Cowes on the Isle of Wight to see the preliminary races of Cowes Week, and to view the boats and the celebrities crowded into Cowes harbour from the four corners of the world. The larger boats always spilled out into the rougher waters of Cowes Roads, creating a splendid sight, and Toby was looking forward to it.

The wind was against them, which meant tacking across the short stretch of water that lay between the mainland and the Isle of Wight. Then, as often before, Naomi wondered how the Island could look so near from the safety of the land, but when one was actually sailing, it could be so far away and take so long! She hated tacking, having to throw oneself from one side of the boat to the other, ducking to avoid the leeward jib as it flew across, while the bow of the boat passed through the eye of the wind.

But Toby loved it. He waited with excited anticipation as soon as he heard Bob's shouted command, 'Ready about!' and then threw himself with gusto at the cry 'Lee-oh!'

He had a fearless, reckless love of the sea, and seemed to thrive on the scent of danger. Although Naomi hated it, she still felt happier being with Toby, rather than letting him go out alone with Bob and Janet.

Although it was August the wind was icy, and

grew stronger and stronger. 'Better put on the safety lines.' Janet's voice was faint, as she shouted the instruction through cupped hands at Naomi.

She nodded, and reached towards the lines with numbed, cold fingers, ready to clip one on to the belt around Toby's lifejacket, when the unthinkable happened.

'Ready about—lee-oh!' Bob's voice was torn to shreds and tossed away by the wind.

Both Naomi and Toby moved automatically, but Toby was faster than Naomi, and as the boat fell away on to the new tack, so Toby disappeared over the side. Naomi wasn't even aware that she'd screamed, as without thinking she hurled herself into the dark grey waters of the heaving Solent. Her eyes were fixed on the bright orange of Toby's lifejacket as it bobbed rapidly away, being swallowed out of sight every other second by huge waves.

Afterwards she was never really sure what had happened. It seemed a lifetime, and yet at the same time everything happened at once. Gulping in great mouthfuls of acrid sea water, mountainous waves buffeting her about, and the orange of Toby's lifejacket getting further and further away, she felt her end had come, when suddenly a great roaring sound filled her ears, and a huge red monster from the deep appeared from nowhere. She was hauled up coughing and choking, and dumped unceremoniously beside Toby on the deck of an enormous power-boat. Apart from a few coughs and splutters, Toby seemed none the worse for the ordeal, and immediately began to shriek excitedly that this was the biggest power-boat he'd ever seen.

With a gasp of relief Naomi hugged Toby to her, only to be brushed aside. He was much more interested in talking to the two men who had rescued them. As far as he was concerned he'd got a ducking, nothing more, he was too young to know his life had been in dire danger.

'That was a bloody silly thing to do—one man overboard is bad enough, but to have another jump is suicide!'

The voice was familiar, the tone familiar. Still coughing up sea water, Naomi raised her head and stared into the eyes that had been haunting her dreams the whole week. Eyes as dark and stormy as the waters of the ocean around them.

'What on earth——?' she began.

'Exactly! What on earth made you do it?'

'I went in after Toby.'

'I could see that. A devastating piece of female logic if every I heard it. What exactly did you hope to achieve, a double obituary?'

Naomi gritted her teeth and clenched her fists. Everything that had happened seemed like some terrible nightmare, and then to be plucked from the sea by Luke Roderick was just too incredible to believe. Perhaps it was a nightmare, and in a minute she'd wake up and find it had never happened. But the feel of a strong hand on her shoulder shaking her vigorously assured her she was awake. It really had happened, and now here was Luke castigating her for her stupidity.

'You're in shock,' he said roughly. 'He isn't.'
He nodded towards Toby, who by now was
standing by the other man at the wheel, waving
excitedly to Bob and Janet, who were signalling
frantically that they were carrying on across to the
Island.

'Perhaps you could give us a lift to Cowes,' said
Naomi with a gulp, wiping some of the salt water
from her face.

'Do we have a choice?' came the uncompro-
mising answer.

'Well, you could always dump us back in the sea,
I suppose,' she muttered ungraciously.

Luke grinned suddenly. 'If you don't behave
yourself, I might very well do just that. You and
your . . . er . . .' he looked over questioningly
towards Toby.

'My nephew, Toby,' said Naomi, looking
lovingly at the small boy standing beside the
helmsman, and then back to Luke.

'You're a very devoted aunt, I'll give you that
much,' said Luke.

But Naomi was hardly listening, she was looking
from Toby to Luke, and back again. The strangest
thing had just struck her. There was the most
uncanny resemblance between Luke and Toby; in
spite of the enormous gap in years they could have
been brothers—dark, crisp hair, clear-cut features
and the same sea-green eyes. It was uncanny, and
she shivered violently.

'As soon as we get on dry land you've both got

to get out of those wet things,' said Luke, noticing
the shiver.

CHAPTER SIX

JANET and Bob were very dear friends, but they did have what Naomi considered to be an absolutely maddening habit of taking over and organising everything. For herself, she would have been more than happy to have said a polite thank you for being hauled out of the drink, and then to have made her own arrangements for the rest of the day. But Janet and Bob, Luke and his fellow sailor, whose name was Matt, colluded together. They had other ideas.

Matt, it transpired, was living in the old tide mill at Maltsworth, the next village along the coast from Longstone, and when she found out, Janet lost no time in getting acquainted. Naomi knew very well why—Janet was very keen on local history, and had always said how much she'd been longing to get inside the mill now it had been restored. Now she had met the man living there, she took it as a golden opportunity not to be missed.

So before Naomi had a chance to demur, the whole party had descended upon some friends of Matt, who by coincidence also happened to be sailing acquaintances of Bob and Janet. After explanations and cries of welcome, they had set about organising lunch, and Naomi knew she was trapped. She forced herself to smile gratefully, but silently cursed the fact that now she would have to spend a whole day in the company of the very disturbing man she'd been trying to avoid all week. Toby, of course, was over the moon. Surrounded by people talking about boats and engines, he was in his element. That was another problem, Naomi thought moodily, the matter of Toby. All the years of carefully preserving her private life as a separate entity from work had vanished like spray before the wind. Why did fate have to deal her such a card? Why did it have to be her boss, the newest member of Accident and Emergency, to find out?

But perhaps it's just as well, Naomi tried to tell herself as she briskly towelled herself dry in her host's bathroom. If Luke knows I have a small boy in my care, the slight attraction he's felt will disappear, the way it always has with other men, and I shall be left in peace once more. But do you want that? her subconscious probed, relentless and searching, do you want a sterile barren life for ever? Life with Luke Roderick around wouldn't be sterile, that much she knew, it would be full, passionate and throbbing with life. Better to have loved and lost than never to have loved at all, the quotation came into her mind.

'What are you thinking of, you stupid girl?' she whispered out loud, staring at her wide-eyed reflection in the bathroom mirror. 'You're pretending something exists between you and Luke when nothing does. Wishful thinking, reading something into a mere hug and a little kiss. Something he hasn't even given a second thought!'

She shrugged on a borrowed navy sweater and jeans, much too large for her slender frame, and tying her gold-streaked hair back in a ponytail, which had the effect of making her look about seventeen, went downstairs, determined to be sensible and not let her over-active imagination run away with her. It was essential she should keep Luke Roderick, the man with the dangerously charismatic aura, in proper perspective.

Toby hardly paid Naomi more than a passing glance. He was excited and happy, listening intently, and joining avidly in the conversation. He couldn't hear enough about the power-boat that had plucked them from the deep—the engine, the horsepower, fuel consumption. Everything about it fascinated him.

'He's a very bright little lad,' Luke remarked to Naomi, when she rejoined the party knitted out in her borrowed clothes. His eyes flickered appreciatively over the slender line of her neck emphasised by her hair drawn back in the ponytail. 'His mother must be very proud of him,' he added.

Naomi took a deep breath. The questions had started, the inevitable questions. 'His mother is dead,' she said quietly.

'And his father?'

'No father either, I'm afraid,' she replied after a fraction of a second's hesitation, adding in a voice that didn't invite further queries, 'I've been aunt and substitute mother and father to him for most of his life.'

The assembled company was drinking hot soup, crowded around a scrubbed pine table in the large kitchen overlooking Cowes harbour. Naomi studiously avoided Luke's penetrating gaze, and stared out of the window as if the serried masts of the boats bobbing and swaying in the wind was the most fascinating sight she'd ever seen.

'Ah, that explains a lot,' said Luke softly.

'Explains what?' Naomi looked at him, frowning across the rim of her steaming mug.

'Your hostile reaction to my remarks on the question of one-parent families. It was because you're bringing him up on your own.'

'You've jumped to the wrong conclusion, I'm afraid,' she answered, trying to be cool, but feeling on the defensive. Trust him to home in right on to the point! But she was damned if she was going to give him the satisfaction of knowing it was something she did worry about. Although why she should feel so illogically stubborn she wasn't sure, it was as though some sixth sense was telling her to keep quiet. Strange undercurrents seemed to swirl about her, telling her that in some way Luke threatened her relationship with Toby.

'Toby may not have a father or mother,' she said sharply, 'but as you can see, he's far from neglected, and also I'm not bringing him up on my own. He has another aunt, an elderly one, Aunt Flo who he lives with all week, and she's a very comforting and constant factor in his life.'

'He needs a man,' said Luke, looking across

at Toby, who was engaged in animated conversation with Matt.

Matt, Naomi gathered from the snippets of conversation she had picked up, was something to do with high-powered engines, and Toby, to her utter amazement, seemed to know an awful lot about such things.

'We get on just fine without a man,' she snapped, annoyed at Luke's remark, because yet again he was echoing her own underlying doubts. Anyway, she told herself crossly, shooting him a vexed glance, it was nothing to do with him.

'You should get married.'

Choking on a mouthful of hot soup, Naomi stared at him, her tawny eyes wide in astonishment. What a nerve the man had! Suddenly she felt furious. He could be as dominating as he liked in the hospital, but outside, he should mind his own damned business!

'A very good idea,' she said sarcastically, when she'd managed to gulp down the soup, scalding her mouth in the process, 'and what do you propose I should do? Put a note on the notice board saying I'm open to offers?'

'That's one way, I suppose,' he smiled lazily, 'but you could—' he paused a moment, then said with a calculated nonchalance, 'start the ball rolling by making yourself more agreeable to men.' He leaned forward, his green eyes fixing her with a mesmerising stare. 'Of course,' he continued silkily, 'I have noticed on one or two occasions that you can be *quite* agreeable.' Naomi flushed, knowing instinctively that he was referring to the times she had been in his arms. 'But unfortunately,' he continued smoothly, 'you seem incapable of keeping it up!'

Naomi's eyes sparkled angrily. 'I am agreeable,' she said, adding pointedly through clenched teeth, 'to *most* men!'

'Oh yes, I'd forgotten Richard Nicholas. But isn't he a little too young to take on the responsibility of a family?'

'I'm not looking for anyone to take me on, as you put it,' said Naomi, 'and merely because you rescued us, don't presume to think it gives you any right to comment on my private life.' She could feel her cheeks beginning to burn as her temper rose, and turned her chair slightly so that she needn't face him. She tried to join in the general conversation and ignore Luke, who, she could see out of the corner of her eye, was smiling in a galling fashion through narrowed quizzical eyes.

But the conversation didn't help raise her lowered spirits much. Everything was conspiring against her. Matt had already invited Bob and Janet to the mill at Maltsworth the following weekend, and Toby wanted to go as well. They were to look at the other two power-boats kept in the boathouse there. And to cap it all, Naomi heard with dismay that Matt had promised that he and Luke would take Toby to a motor race meeting at Silverstone the weekend after that.

'Of course, we'd love you to come too,' Matt said Naomi. 'This young lad of yours has definitely got a flare for engines, there's not much he doesn't know.'

'So I've gathered during the last half hour,' said Naomi, smiling.

It was impossible not to like Matt. He was inclined to plumpness, balding, and what hair he had left was silver. But he had twinkling blue eyes, a round cheerful face, and a distinctly fatherly air about him. Perhaps that was the answer—Toby needed a friend like that, a father figure who could also be her friend. With a fillip of smug satisfaction, Naomi decided to cultivate the friendship with Matt. Luke was wrong, she didn't need to marry to find a man for Toby!

Manoeuvring herself so that her back was facing Luke, she let the conversation swirl about her. Everyone was talking at once, more hot soup was dished out and hunks torn out of fresh French bread; the chatter of voices never flagging for a moment. Matt, she found out, was a widower with two grown-up sons, one of whom was an aspiring racing driver, hence the visit to Silverstone, she supposed. But she didn't ask, just sat and listened, and tried to ignore the man sitting close behind her. Although she could almost physically feel his eyes boring into her back, and had a very good idea of his expression. Sardonic amusement at her discomfiture!

But she couldn't escape Luke's company, not even when the party split up. It was decided that she and Toby should be taken back to Longstone in the power-boat.

'I think you two will be safer with us,' Luke had said firmly, looking at the heaving waters of the Solent.

Toby was overjoyed, and secretly Naomi was relieved too. Anything was better than sailing back in a gale, although she would have preferred it if just Matt had been there. All heads in Cowes turned their way as the huge red boat, with its eight exhaust pipes belching forth heat from the huge engine, purred its way at regulation speed out of the harbour. Once outside Matt let out the throttle, and they sliced through the water at breakneck speed. Toby was in the seventh heaven, and watching him as he stood beside Luke, Naomi noticed that they even had the same expression, one of dedicated, suppressed excitement.

For the rest of the evening, after they'd said goodbye to Luke and Matt and had watched them roar off in the direction of Maltsworth, she and Aunt Flo had heard nothing from Toby but quotations of Matt and Luke.

'And to think, dear, that you work with this Luke,' said Aunt Flo. 'That's nice, isn't it?'

'Yes,' said Naomi gloomily, wishing she could say what she really felt, that it was anything but nice, and that she felt disturbed and worried. But common sense told her that it was ridiculous to feel worried; there was nothing to worry about. So why was it she couldn't shake off the feeling? Toby was still talking about the prospect of the weekends ahead when she kissed him a tender goodnight, before setting off on her journey back to the lonely

Not just a token... a real gift for you

This 2-part glass oyster dish is **FREE** together with a surprise mystery gift for every reader who decides to sample the Temptation Experience.

Exquisitely modelled to add a pretty touch to your sitting room, hall or bedroom – these two dishes fit together elegantly like a genuine oyster shell. Both gifts come absolutely FREE if you fill in the claim card and post it off today for your four free Temptation novels.

Yes Please send me, free and without obligation, four Temptation novels, together with my free glass dishes and mystery gift – and reserve a Reader Service subscription for me. If I decide to subscribe I shall receive four new books every month for just £5.00 – post and packing free. If I decide not to subscribe I shall write to you within 10 days. The free books and gifts are mine to keep in any case.

I understand that I may cancel or suspend my subscription at any time simply by writing to you. I am over 18 years of age.

PLEASE WRITE IN BLOCK CAPITALS   2A9T

Name_____

Address_____

_____

_____ Postcode_____

Signature _____
Are you already a Reader Service subscriber? YES ☐   NO ☐
If you are, you can still receive Temptation in addition to your existing subscription.

Mills & Boon Ltd reserve the right to exercise discretion in granting membership and to change the terms of this offer. Overseas – please send for details. You may be mailed with other offers as a result of this application. Offer expires June 30th 1989.

Yes Please send me my FOUR FREE TEMPTATION NOVELS as soon as possible, without any charges for post and packing.

Yes I would also like to receive a 2-part glass oyster dish and a surprise mystery gift.

Yes Please reserve a Reader Service subscription for me so that I can enjoy all these benefits with no obligation to purchase a minimum number of books

- free newsletter packed with author news, free competitions, previews and special book offers

- free postage and packing

- the latest titles reserved for me and delivered direct to my door

Remember, your Free Gifts and your Four Free Temptation novels are yours to keep without obligation!

Reader Service
FREEPOST
PO Box 236
Croydon
SURREY
CR9 9EL.

NO
STAMP
NEEDED.

bed-sit near the County General.

'You will come to the mill to see the boats, and to the motor racing, won't you?' he asked.

'Of course, if you want me to,' Naomi smiled. She couldn't spoil his enjoyment merely because she found Luke disturbing. Anyway, Luke hadn't said he'd be at the mill, so that was one weekend she didn't have to worry about.

'Oh yes,' murmured Toby sleepily, the exciting events of the day beginning to catch up with him, 'Luke and Matt said they wanted you to come, Luke said . . .' His eyes closed and he was asleep.

'Luke said, Luke said.' The words hammered through Naomi's brain all the way back towards the County General, vibrating in time to the revs of the engine.

It seemed her premonitions were coming true. Luke was getting involved in her life, hers and Toby's. But firmly she checked her wayward thoughts and told herself that she was overwrought and tired. Spending one day of a weekend with Luke at the races was hardly getting involved. He wasn't going to be at the mill, Matt had issued the invitation, not Luke. She was being stupid again.

But remnants of unease were still there, lurking in her mind, when she awoke the following morning. Stop being stupid, she told herself crossly, as she struggled through her usual morning routine. She showered, grabbed a quick yoghourt and donned the crisp pale blue uniform, encircled her waist with the deep purple belt denoting her status as a staff nurse, and topped it off with a pristine white, freshly laundered frilly cap, pinned to her neatly tied back hair.

Setting off in the early morning sunshine for the short walk towards the huge building that was the County General, she told herself very firmly that a spell of hard work would soon dispense with all her far-flung and ridiculous notions—such as Luke Roderick being able to have any influence on her private life. He was her boss, nothing more.

Looking forward to hard work, however, did not prepare Naomi, or anyone else in A and E, for the onslaught which overtook them that morning. As a department, they had often practised their part of the hospital's Major Incident Plan, with imaginary disasters planned out by administrators, but they'd never actually been put to the test by having to cope with a real one.

So when the call came through to the nurses' changing room that the hospital had been put on 'red alert', it was greeted with the usual degree of urgency and enthusiasm such exercises aroused.

'On a Monday morning too,' wailed Gloria, late on duty as usual. 'And I haven't even had time to put on my mascara yet. I can't go out with no eyes!'

'You'll have to,' grinned Naomi unsympathetically, dragging a reluctant Gloria after her. 'I wonder what they've dreamed up for us this time.'

Gloria followed, grumbling crossly that she didn't care, but whatever it was she couldn't face anyone without her eyes made up! But at the sight of a grim-faced Luke and Sister Murphy waiting for them, even her protests faded away. This, quite obviously, was not an exercise, this was the real thing.

After making sure that all his team were present, Luke told the assembled company what information he had. 'There's been a chemical spillage from a parked tanker. Seven thousand five hundred litres of an unknown chemical has seeped out from a split valve during the night. Unfortunately the lorry was parked right in the centre of a large housing estate, and noxious fumes have slowly spread over part of the estate throughout the night. We don't know the nature of the chemical at the moment, so treatment is going to be difficult. The first cases will be here any moment.'

'Do you know the symptoms the patients will be presenting with?' asked Patrick Rogers.

'The ambulance crews and police have informed me that it's vomiting, lightheadedness, headaches, sore eyes, nausea and respiratory problems. We'll treat the obvious symptoms first, and as soon as I get an update on the actual chemical or chemicals involved, then I'll tell you if we need to revise our treatment.'

The words were hardly out of his mouth before the first of a fleet of ambulances arrived. The hospital's Major Incident Plan moved swiftly into top gear, and Naomi, along with the rest of the team, was glad of the exercises they'd grumbled about so often. Now they could all see it was paying off. No one needed to ask what to do, they all knew who they had to work with, how to sort out the patients into degrees of severity from the treatment point of view, and who to telephone for back-up when necessary.

Richard appeared by Naomi's side, called back from his study leave for the emergency. Together they and Swaroop Rao worked as a team.

Richard and Naomi did a full physical examination of the patients, sending those complaining of the most severe discomfort on breathing for chest X-ray, giving anti-emetics to those complaining of nausea and then passing them all on to Swaroop, who had instructions to wash out every patient's eyes thoroughly with methyl-cellulose eye-drops. None of the patients they saw was severely ill, just very uncomfortable. But it was the actual volume of patients that very nearly overwhelmed them.

'When are they going to stop coming?' asked Richard as an ambulance crew escorted another six patients, all coughing and wiping their streaming eyes, into the bay where they were working.

'Should be about the last of them,' replied the ambulance man, who looked as if he was kitted out for space travel in his protective clothing.

At that moment Luke joined them in the treatment cubicle, and from his expression Naomi could see at once that he was relieved. 'You'll be glad to know the stuff we've been dealing with is not badly toxic. Luckily by tomorrow, for most of the patients, this will just be a bad memory.'

'What was it?' asked Richard.

'A mixture of isopropyl alcohol, methanol, acetone, potassium, sulphur, water and salts,' said Luke, consulting a piece of paper. 'Apparently on its way to a waste disposal plant.'

'Sounds awful to me,' spluttered one of the patients from his prone position on the couch. 'Are you sure we'll be OK, Doctor?'

'Don't worry about it,' Naomi soothed the anxious patient. 'You've inhaled a pretty nasty cocktail, but if Mr Roderick says you'll be all right, then you will be.'

'Thanks for the vote of confidence, Nurse,' said Luke in a low voice, raising one quizzical eyebrow as he smiled for the first time that morning. 'A nasty cocktail, that's a good description. I must remember that when I'm writing up this morning's events.' With that he was gone to tell the good news to the other teams still beavering away with their patients in adjoining treatment cubicles.

About three-quarters of an hour later they had finished. They had worked right through the day, missing coffee break and lunch break. But by now most of the patients had gone home, and of the total of seventy patients actually treated in Casualty, only six had been detained for overnight observation. These had all been respiratory problems, and had been shipped off to the wards to be looked after by the chest physicians.

The A and E team involved in the major incident collectively slumped down exhausted in the coffee lounge of the hospital canteen, where a late lunch had been laid on for them. Another team had been brought in by the hospital administration to run Casualty for the rest of the afternoon, and Luke told the morning team they could all take the rest of the day off.

'What there is left of it,' grumbled Richard, squashed in beside Naomi and tucking into shepherd's pie and chips. 'I'll never be able to get down to studying again today, my brain just won't function properly.'

Naomi agreed absentmindedly. She had her shoes off as usual, and was wondering how on earth she would get through waitressing that night. Already she felt so tired it was an effort to put one foot in front of another, but somehow she knew she would have to manage.

Richard finished his lunch and stood up. 'I've got to love you and leave you,' he announced to no one in particular. 'Got to hit the books again.'

'Go on, Richard, you'll pass easily,' teased Gloria. 'You'll soon be an FRCS and then you too can be head of an A and E department.'

'Even if I pass, which I doubt, that exalted position won't be mine for another five or six years,' said Richard, determined to be pessimistic. He shuffled out of the confined space sideways, and in doing so kicked Naomi's shoes out from under the table, right into the centre of the room in full view of everyone.

'Oh Richard,' groaned Naomi, 'look what you've done!'

'Never mind, Sir Galahad is coming to the

rescue,' he muttered unrepentantly, as Luke got up quickly and retrieved the shoes.

'Here.' Luke handed the shoes back to Naomi and slid his long form down into the seat vacated by Richard.

Naomi took them and started to push her reluctant feet back into the shoes, uncomfortably aware of Luke's penetrating gaze taking in her every move.

'Why don't you get yourself a pair of shoes that are big enough?' he asked.

'Why don't you mind your own business?' She felt frayed at the edges already, without having someone tell her she needed bigger shoes!

'I've half a mind to throw them out of the window so that you *have* to buy another pair.' At Naomi's horrified gasp he threw back his head and roared with deep-throated laughter. 'Don't worry, I won't. I can't have one of my staff nurses walking through the hospital barefoot.'

By now most of the rest of the A and E staff were drifting off in twos and threes, and Naomi longed to make her escape too. But her route was blocked by the very solid form of Luke Roderick, who looked as if he intended sitting there for the rest of the afternoon.

'I'm going now, Luke.' Rose Murphy waddled over, her usual ruddy complexion quite pallid from the unexpected exertion of the morning. 'Is there anything else you want before I go?'

'Not unless you can find me some gorgeous maiden to ravish,' said Luke wickedly.

'You'll have to make do with Naomi,' said Sister Murphy with an unusual flash of humour.

'I'm not in the mood to be ravished,' said Naomi pertly. 'Excuse me.' She tried to edge past Luke, but he'd already signalled to the canteen managress, who was on her way over with another pot of coffee.

'Well, if I can't ravish you, at least have another coffee. There's no hurry, is there? Not unless you're going off to buy a bigger pair of shoes!'

'No, I am *not*!' said Naomi vehemently.

'Where's your sense of humour?' he asked with a wry twist of the lips. He slid his arm casually along the back of her seat, his long fingers teasing idly with a loose stand of her silky hair. 'There's nothing wrong with having big feet,' he added, which as far as Naomi was concerned was nothing more than heaping insult upon injury.

'My feet are not big,' she said hotly, 'and I don't want another cup of coffee, thank you, I'd much prefer to go off duty.'

'Ah yes, rushing off to wherever it is you always do rush off to,' said Luke slowly, not attempting to remove his hand.

Naomi moved uncomfortably in her seat, trying to ignore the tingling sensation running up and down her spine, annoyed at her capricious body for responding so readily to his touch. She caught his gaze and turned away quickly. His eyes had such a searching quality, almost as if he could look right into her head and see her innermost thoughts.

'Who did you say Toby's father was?' The

suddenness of the question unnerved her.

'I . . . er . . . I didn't.' She found herself stumbling over the words.

'Who was he?' The words, so innocent in themselves, struck into Naomi's heart like icy needles. With a sudden flash of insight she knew that this was why she'd kept Toby's existence hidden from her friends. She'd never truly wanted to face up to the fact that Toby even *had* a father.

She looked down at her feet in their too-tight shoes, anguishing over what to say, hating herself for what she was about to do, lie to Luke; but there seemed no alternative.

'I don't know who the father is,' she said at last, in a voice barely above a whisper, trying to persuade herself that it was the truth, or at least almost the truth.

'You don't know?' Luke sounded incredulous.

'No,' Naomi hesitated, she had to say more than that. 'I have an idea,' she said at last, the words dragging out reluctantly, 'but I can't be sure, so I've never done anything about it.'

'I would never have believed it of you—you of all people.' Luke leaned forward as he spoke.

Startled at the strangeness of his words, Naomi raised her head and looked at him. What she saw in the dark depths of his eyes was a deep compassion. Suddenly it took all her self-control not to burst into hysterical laughter. The irony of it struck her forcibly—Luke thought she was Toby's mother, not his aunt! Here she was, her long-dormant feeling of latent womanhood suddenly aroused by Luke; Naomi Selbourne, a virgin, untried and unsure of her self, but in Luke's eyes an unmarried mother!

CHAPTER SEVEN

HIS VERY NEXT words confirmed that her suspicions were true.

'Look, Naomi, I don't want to pry, but have you ever thought of having a blood test to determine Toby's paternity?'

To make matters worse, he reached over and gently captured her hands in his. At the touch of his hands Naomi felt herself begin to tremble, and tried to look away. The serious tone of his voice, together with the compassionate searching gaze in the submarine depths of his eyes, brought on a disturbing flutter in the pit of her stomach. She'd never particularly cared what men had thought about her relationship with Toby before, in fact she's hardly given it any thought at all. But now it struck her forcibly that she did care what Luke thought, she cared very, very much indeed.

But in spite of that fact, she still couldn't bring herself to blurt out the truth, not even to Luke. That would be traitorous to Tiffany's memory, and Naomi believed fiercely that her sister deserved dignity in death. Tiffany couldn't defend herself. Naomi was the only one who could. It was far better for everyone if she maintained the discreet silence she'd always maintained. Better for everyone, that was, except herself.

'Here, have another coffee,' said Luke, his voice deepening with a tenderness that made Naomi's throat ache. He stilled her trembling hands. 'There's no need to react like this. You're not the first girl it's happened to.'

This was getting worse and worse! I bet he's thinking most girls have some idea of their child's father, thought Naomi miserably. He really must be thinking she'd done the rounds! But still she remained obstinately silent, and pulling her hand from his to pick up a cup of coffee, tried to control her shaking limbs and not let the cup rattle too much in the saucer. One thought beat insistently through her mind, and that was that she had to get away from Luke. Get away, before she got in too deep, and told too many lies. There was nothing she could do but let Luke believe his assumption was correct—let him believe she was Toby's mother. But she was skating on thin ice, and suddenly she realised how vulnerable she was. A few more kind words, and she'd be blurting out the story about Tiffany and Dirk Roderigues.

Gulping down the rest of the hot coffee in one mouthful, she rose unsteadily to her feet. 'I really must go,' she said firmly, her voice echoing a tranquillity that belied her inner turmoil.

'But we haven't discussed the possibilities,' began Luke. 'I think . . .'

'There's nothing I wish to discuss,' said Naomi unwaveringly, the coiled tenseness within her adding a sharp edge to her voice. 'And although

I'm sure you mean well,' she added, 'there's no need to concern yourself with my affairs. I can look after myself *and* Toby.'

'But I like Toby. In a strange way I feel as if I've known him before,' said Luke, a puzzled note to his voice. 'It's very strange,' he added, almost as a second thought to himself.

'Yes, it is strange,' agreed Naomi, adding with a brittle laugh, 'but at least I know *you're* not the father!'

As soon as she'd uttered the words she immediately wished she hadn't. She could have bitten out her tongue with remorse, but it seemed as if some inner devil was driving her on, not only to mask the truth but to purposely drive Luke away.

'Now if you'll excuse me,' she added, this time not waiting for him to move, but pushing past forcibly, 'I really *am* going off duty.'

A hand at the end of a steel ramrod of an arm shot out and clamped around her wrist. 'Haven't you ever thought of the effect this could have on Toby?' Luke said brusquely.

Vainly Naomi tried to wrench her hand away, but it was a hopeless ineffectual struggle against his massive strength. As she glanced down at his imprisoning hand, twice the size of hers, the memory of the pirate on the front of Sister Murphy's book flashed across her mind. It certainly felt, from the pressure on her wrist, as if Luke would have the strength to fight his way out of any situation, tear a man in two if he were so minded.

The thought of his masculine strength pitted against her femininity suddenly served to enrage her. The tumult of conflicting emotions raging inside her exploded. 'Let go of me, you big bully!' she snapped. Temper goaded her on to recklessness. 'And please forget about the next couple of weekends. I've no wish to spend any of my free time with you or your friends. I've quite enough to do without voluntarily submitting myself to a replay of the Spanish Inquisition!'

'If you do back out, then you don't care as much as you say you do about Toby,' taunted Luke, his face darkening angrily at her words. 'What will you tell him? You don't like me, therefore *he's* not to have any fun!'

'You rotten . . .' His verbal onslaught had struck home, like a sharp-edged blade twisting inside her. He was right, of course, she could't do that. Furiously she tried to wrench her hand from his.

'Don't bother to finish the sentence, I've a pretty good idea of what you were about to say,' he grated.

'I'll honour the arrangement for the planned weekends,' said Naomi on a calmer note, although her heart and mind seethed as a mixture of turbulent emotions jostled for supremacy. 'But after that, I'd be very glad if you stayed right out of my life.'

On the last word she succeeded in jerking her wrist free, and managed to extricate herself from beside Luke, at the same time putting the safety of the table between them. 'I'd be very grateful if you would respect my wish,' she said in a low voice.

But even as she was telling him to stay out of her life, she knew that Luke could be the father Toby needed, and the lover she had unknowingly longed for. The realisation left her feeling weak at the knees, a mixture of raw desire as she looked at Luke's lean features, and anger and frustration at the knowledge that none of this would ever be.

Luke added to the surge of misery overwhelming her with his glacial reply. 'I think you're probably right. I would be wiser to stay out of your life. We seem to mix about as well as oil and water.'

She wanted to cry out, to explain, but the words lodged like hard stones in her throat. Unshed tears stinging the back of her eyelids, she turned swiftly away and left the canteen. The canteen manageress wondered what on earth had happened to cause Luke Roderick to sit alone at the table, staring into his coffee his face thunderous, his mouth set in an uncompromisingly stubborn line.

In spite of being tired Naomi was glad of the work at the Water's Edge that night, it took her mind from the immediate problems of Luke and Toby. Luke and Toby, that was how she found herself thinking, and try as she might she found it difficult to separate the two. As the evening wore on she began to think more and more that she'd been a stupid fool to let Luke go on thinking she was Toby's mother. A golden opportunity to tell him the truth had presented itself, and she had ignored it. It was too late to backtrack now. He'd only think it was something she had dreamed up in an effort to redeem her character in his eyes, and she couldn't blame him for that! She smiled a sad, rueful smile. She'd made her bed, as the saying went, and now she had no alternative but to lie on it!

'Good heavens, dearie, you've got the wind behind you tonight all right,' said Molly as Naomi whizzed into the kitchen with yet another pile of plates in her arms. 'You've taken more orders than anyone else. I don't know where you get your energy from.'

'Nervous energy,' said Naomi with a laugh. But the laughter rang hollow in her ears. Nervous energy—how true that was! She had a feeling that if she didn't stop running something dreadful would catch up with her, although what that something was she couldn't have put into words, but she had a notion it had something to do with Luke.

So she worked on, driving herself to the limits of her physical ability, automatically taking orders, clearing tables, washing glasses, anything to ensure there was not an idle moment in the evening. But even so, she couldn't escape her mind, and found herself mulling over the possibility of changing hospitals. That would be one way, she reasoned, of avoiding contact with Luke. She knew she could always find work at St Rosemary's further along the coast, but that would also mean finding another part-time job to make up the extra money. Reluctantly she had to admit that she was unlikely to get another hospital to accept the hours she wanted, or another job as good as the one at the Water's Edge.

Even though exhausted she couldn't escape her thoughts when she laid her head on the pillow that night. Every time she closed her eyes she could see Luke's face wearing the expression that had told her so clearly that he was sure she was Toby's real mother.

As she eventually fell into an uneasy sleep, her last lingering thought was dreading the advent of dawn, and the time she'd have to face Luke once more.

The following morning dawned grey and gloomy, a fine mist of drizzle dampening everything. A typically wet English summer's day, which shed its mantle of depression over everyone, the members of A and E being no exception. The whole place reeked with an air of gloom and despondency in tune with the weather. To Naomi's finely keened senses it seemed Luke was more abrupt with her than with anyone else, and although she tried to pay no attention, she felt hurt and unhappy. I ought to be pleased, she told herself sternly, it's what I told him I wanted, to be left alone. So why was it she felt hopelessly depressed when his icy glance swept dismissively past her?

But as the morning wore on, her natural good humour surfaced, coming to her rescue as it had done so often in the past when things had looked black.

She had a wicked sense of the ridiculous, and now she mused wryly that perhaps she ought to be wearing a red uniform instead of a blue one. He's obviously relegated me to the position of scarlet woman, she thought, mentally pulling a face at the back of his broad shoulders. That surely must account for the stony-faced glance he had thrown in her direction.

Not that he was in any position to make moral judgements, if the articles in the newspaper gossip columns were anything to go by. When he'd been doing his TV series there had been some titbit of information about him every day. She recalled one headline, 'The surgeon with a girl in every port', which referred to the fact that whenever his ship touched land, some glamorous female had managed to fly out, or even in one celebrated case a famous model had travelled by camel in order to be there to greet him when he set foot on dry land.

So play at being self-righteous, Naomi thought acrimoniously, when Luke had walked past her and closeted himself in his office, and I hope it does your ego good! For a moment or two she wished she really had been a good-time girl, at least then she'd have some exciting memories. As it is, she thought morosely, my life is about as exciting as a suet pudding!

'Mr Roderick's writing a research paper,' said Sister Murphy in answer to Patrick's query. 'He said you'll have to manage on your own this morning unless a dire emergency comes in.'

Patrick groaned and Naomi and Gloria ex-

changed glances. It hadn't taken them long to
discover that their locum, Patrick Rogers, wasn't
over-fond of hard work, and took whatever
opportunity he could find to get out of it. And
what was even more infuriating, somehow
contrived never to get caught. Unlike poor
Richard, who wasn't half as devious, and never
managed to get away with anything.

'Oh, this wretched weather!' moaned Gloria,
stopping for a moment beside Naomi, who was
attempting to sort out a pile of X-rays, left in a
hopeless muddle by Patrick in his usual cavalier
fashion. 'I think I'll resign,' she said suddenly,
'and apply for a job in Italy.'

'You speak Italian?' Naomi was surprised.

'Not a word,' said Gloria blithely, 'but this,' she
pointed towards the window at the steady stream
of drizzle falling from the grey skies outside, 'is a
distinct incentive to learn!'

'Yes, you're right,' agreed Naomi, looking
wistfully out of the window as Gloria walked away.
'It would be lovely to get away,' she added under
her breath.

'Running away from things, especially
something like the truth, never gets you anywhere.
It will always catch up with you,' Luke's voice said
quietly behind her.

'As usual you butt into someone's private
conversation, and jump to completely the wrong
conclusion,' said Naomi sharply. What a nerve the
man had—once he got the bit between his teeth it
seemed, like the British bulldog, he would never

let go! Well, two could play at that game. Neither would she. Her golden eyes blazed as she turned to face him. She had asked him to stay out of her life, he had no right to barge in where he wasn't wanted. 'Isn't he wanted?' an irksome little voice taunted, repeating and repeating from somewhere within the depths of her subconscious. Naomi firmly suppressed it, and continued. 'I happened to be talking to Gloria,' she said coldly, 'and we were discussing the weather!'

'I wasn't,' he replied, not deviating one iota from his point.

For one moment Naomi was tempted to pick up the X-rays and bring them down with an almighty thump across his black, arrogant head, but then sober reason prevailed. Sister Murphy might notice, then she really would be looking for another job!

'I thought we'd agreed that my private life was my own,' she muttered.

'I don't remember agreeing to anything,' he replied.

'Isn't there a course or something you can take to help your memory? I'm sure I've seen it advertised in the Sunday supplements.'

'There's no need to be flippant.'

'It's the only way I know of controlling the almost irresistible urge I have to strangle you,' said Naomi, keeping her voice bland with an effort, and pinning a determinedly sweet smile on her lips. Out of the corner of her eye she could see Rose Murphy's bulk bearing down upon them.

'This is obviously not the right time or place to continue this conversation,' came the reply, as Luke too spied Rose's size twenty-four dark blue uniform looming ever nearer.

'There will never be a right time or place,' replied Naomi deliberately. A feeling of desolation swept over her. With every word she uttered she was pushing Luke further and further away, but she held her head high and proud. She didn't need his pity or his help.

Sister Murphy drew him away towards her office, and Naomi turned back to her task of sorting the X-rays. Mind your own business, please, Luke she thought miserably, no matter how noble your motives. Her stomach felt knotted with tension. Oh, what a tangled web we weave, she mused, and the most ridiculous part of all was that she couldn't rationalise about her feelings for Luke. All she knew was the fact that she was undeniably attracted to him, in a way she had been to no other man before, and yet at the same time she felt he threatened her. She sighed. What a muddle life was sometimes!

It came as a pleasant surprise that the rest of the afternoon passed by without incident. Not only did Luke not mention anything concerning Toby again, but he was pleasantly friendly, behaving as if nothing had ever happened, and that their conversations had never taken place. Everything appeared to be as it had been right at the very beginning of his time at the County General. There had only been one moment to mar the peace-

fulness of the afternoon, and remind her that Luke
hadn't completely forgotten Toby, and that had
been when Luke and Rose Murphy had tackled her
again about the Sister's post.

'We've had no suitable applicants at all,'
grumbled Sister Murphy.

'And we were wondering whether you would
reconsider,' said Luke, adding casually, 'I know it
doesn't mean much extra money, but surely every
little helps.'

'It has nothing to do with money,' lied Naomi,
wishing she could tell them that working each
evening as a waitress she could earn four times as
much as she'd make as a Sister, without the
additional hassle of a Sister's responsibility.

Luke and Sister had exchanged annoyed glances,
but to Naomi's relief nothing more was said.

'How are we tonight, then?' asked Molly when
Naomi walked into the kitchen and scrambled into
her mini-skirted waitress's uniform in the
cupboard off the kitchen that served as a female
changing room. She eyed herself in the mirror and
pulled a face at her reflection. That was the only
thing she disliked about the job, the wretched
uniform she had to wear. It was much too short for
her, and showed a great deal of her very shapely
long legs—a fact much appreciated by the male
customers. Although over the two years she'd been
waitressing, Naomi had developed an effective
shrivelling glance for any man foolish enough to
make a facile comment.

The first half hour before they opened was when the staff ate, another bonus point as far as Naomi was concerned. It meant she didn't have to spend much money on food in the week. Breakfast was a piece of toast or yoghourt, lunch in the canteen, which was cheap, and a good meal every evening in the kitchen of the Water's Edge.

'I'm fine,' she said in answer to Molly's question, tightening her belt and donning her frilly apron. She sniffed the delicious smell of cooking that filled the kitchen. 'Something smells good.'

'Beef Wellington,' said Molly, putting down a plate of lamp chop, jacket potato and coleslaw in front of Naomi, 'but not for the likes of you and me, I'm afraid!'

'This is good enough to set me up for the evening,' said Naomi gratefully, as she and Molly sat down to eat together. Soon they were joined by the rest of the staff, and plenty of lively banter and gossip was exchanged during their brief respite before the evening rush.

'Fully booked tonight,' said the manager, coming into the kitchen, puffing himself up with importance. A good night's business meant a bonus for him, and plenty of tips for the staff. 'All hands to the pump now, concentration is the name of the game.'

Everyone obediently scurried to their appointed places in the restaurant, to make certain nothing was left unprepared. Mr Moger, the manager, presided over the running of the restaurant as if it was a military operation, and treated everyone as if they were of slightly subnormal intelligence. Sometimes it irritated Naomi, but she pushed it to the back of her mind. She could play as dumb as he wanted just so long as she got the pay packet every night!

Mr Moger had been right, it really was fully booked, in fact overbooked. If one set of customers lingered too long over their coffee and mints, it meant the next party booked in for that table had to wait in the foyer and be entertained with pre-dinner drinks.

It was late in the evening, and everyone was beginning to flag, when Mr Moger came across to Naomi. 'I've just managed to squeeze another party on to one of your tables,' he said. 'A late booking—look after them well.'

Great, thought Naomi with a stab of vexation, it's been a long day, and now I've got to finish it off with a late booking! However, smiling dutifully at Mr Moger, she kept her thoughts to herself, twitched her apron straight and started to walk towards the table where the party of four men for dinner had just been seated.

She'd only taken a few steps when she froze in horror. It couldn't be, not here, not at the Water's Edge! But it was—there was no mistaking that broad back, the familiar set of the muscular shoulders, not even in the dim lighting of the restaurant. It was Luke Roderick, in the company of three other men.

For a moment Naomi was sorely tempted to turn around and run right out of the restaurant there and then, but then the cold logic of resignation took over. She'd always known that sooner or later someone would be bound to find out that she worked in the evenings as a waitress. She would have preferred it to be anyone other than Luke Roderick, but the way her luck was running, it seemed he was destined to find out just about everything there was to know about her!

Taking a deep breath, and hoping her knees didn't actually look as if they were knocking, she started forward and stopped at the table. Taking great care, she placed herself right behind Luke. Like a drowning man clinging to a life raft, she snatched at anything to put off the final moment of discovery. But it seemed her luck was in. One of the men did the ordering, while Luke and the other two men were engaged in deep conversation.

Naomi tried to write down the order, at the same time stealthily concentrating on manoeuvring herself out of Luke's range of vision. The uniform she disliked so much seemed to have shrunk at least six inches in her imagination, and she was more than ever aware of how much leg she revealed.

'Thank you, sir,' she said when she had finished taking the order. She spoke in what she hoped was a disguised voice, deeply husky, nothing at all like her normal tones.

She beat a hasty retreat to the kitchen and breathed a sigh of relief. So far, so good, if only she could persuade someone else to serve at the table she might escape notice. But her luck didn't extend that far. However, by dint of skilful serving, keeping herself just out of Luke's vision by serving him as he turned his head to speak to one of his companions, she managed to serve both the starter and main course without him noticing that the waitress at the table was one of his own staff nurses. Naomi gained in confidence, sure now that she would be able to manage the dessert course in the same manner. And as she'd persuaded Josie, one of the other girls, to do the coffee and mints, she only had the dessert to get through.

The dessert, however, proved to be an insurmountable hurdle. The party went through the menu rejecting everything as unsuitable, and then decided to look at the sweet trolley. The moment Naomi had been hoping to avoid had come. There was no way she could serve from the sweet trolley and stay out of Luke's line of vision, not unless she turned into a contortionist! So, taking a deep breath, she pushed the trolley towards the table. She'd serve Luke first and get it over with.

'What would you like, sir?' she asked, hoping her voice didn't sound as strangled as it felt.

Luke turned and looked her straight in the eye without batting an eyelid in recognition. 'Perhaps you could bring it closer,' he said.

'Yes, sir,' said Naomi in her deep voice, forgetting there was no need for disguise now, and wishing fervently he'd take his eyes off her legs and look at the desserts instead!

'Very nice,' he murmured, still looking at her legs, a smile twitching his lips.

Naomi glowered. 'I recommend the sherry trifle,' she said curtly.

'Then I shall take your advice,' came the imperturbable reply.

At the end of the meal Luke remained behind to pay, and Naomi handed him the bill on a plate in silence. Without looking up he sorted through a sheaf of notes and placed them on the plate, then passed it back to her. Anxious to get away, she started to make her way quickly towards the cash desk, but he stopped her, putting a light but distinctly firm restraining hand on her arm.

'Nice legs,' he drawled slowly, his gaze slowly travelling the length of her long limbs. 'Quite a turn-on for your masculine customers, I'd imagine.'

'I don't know,' said Naomi coldly. 'Most of them are too polite to say anything. This is a high-class restaurant, you know!'

Luke laughed. 'And I particularly liked the bluesy voice,' he continued. 'You're obviously wasted as a staff nurse. You should have been an actress!'

His reward was a glare, as Noami scuttled behind a chair in a vain effort to hide her legs. 'What are you going to do about it, about me working here?' she asked.

'I don't know. I'll think about it.' He glanced across to where his companions were waiting. 'Regrettably, I must go now.'

'You're not going to tell Sister, and get me fired for breaking the rules?' pleaded Noami nervously.

Luke thought for a moment. 'It all depends,' he said.

'On what?'

'I'll let you know when I've thought of something,' came the maddening reply.

CHAPTER EIGHT

WHATEVER it was he had meant by that cryptic remark, by the time she eventually reached her bed-sit and crawled exhausted into bed, Naomi was past caring. She was too tired to care about anything. So she'd been found out at last, the worst had happened, or had it? At that moment in time she was inclined to think that the fact that her car had broken down that night was a much worse catastrophe!

When she tried to leave the restaurant her ancient Renault had stood sullen and silent, refusing point blank to start. No amount of pushing, jump starting or any other trick the head waiter had tried had the slightest effect. At last he had leaned back wearily. 'I think you need a new starter motor,' he announced.

He had been very kind, and gone out of his way to drop her off at the end of her road, but this still meant a long walk up a tree-lined road in the pitch dark. The part of the town where her bed-sit was located was very poorly lit, the old houses big and rambling, surrounded by overgrown gardens. Naomi tried not to be nervous, but at two o'clock in the morning it was very easy to imagine ominous shapes lurking behind every bush. She'd run practically all the way, and landed up on the front porch of the Victorian house where she lived in a hot sweat.

Her first priority the next morning was to telephone the garage and ask them to fix the car. She kept her fingers crossed, hoping it wouldn't be prohibitively expensive; that was the last thing she needed, expensive car repairs. Then it was off to the Accident and Emergency department on tenderhooks, wondering if Luke would mention the previous night.

'Good heavens, Naomi, you look *awful*!' Gloria said the moment she saw her.

'Tact is not one of your stronger points, is it?' Naomi couldn't resist the acid retort.

Swaroop came into the changing room to hang up her cloak, and overheard the exchange of conversation. 'Oh, Gloria,' she said reproachfully, her huge brown eyes full of sympathy for Naomi, 'how can you say such a thing?'

'Because she does look awful,' said Gloria loudly as they left the changing room, determined not to be sidetracked. 'I don't know what you do on your nights off, Naomi, but whatever it is it isn't healthy! I . . . er . . . sorry.'

Busily studying Naomi's face, and not looking where she was going, Gloria had collided straight into the tall form of Luke. It was impossible for him not to have overheard the remark, delivered as it was in Gloria's ringing tones.

Naomi held her breath, waiting for the axe to fall. What would he say? Would he say that she was a waitress at night, and that was the reason she looked so tired? Anxiously her eyes sought out Luke's gaze, silently pleading.

For a moment he swung his stethoscope reflectively between finger and thumb, the green eyes that captured and held Naomi's hypnotized gaze brilliant but impenetrable as agate. It seemed as if he was about to speak, and her heart slumped sickeningly. He was going to tell, and then Rose Murphy would be sure to ask for her resignation. But she had done him an injustice, for after what seemed a lifetime, he merely smiled politely, said, 'Good morning, girls,' and continued on his way in the direction of his office.

Naomi stared at his retreating back, watching the broad shoulders move easily beneath his starched white coat, and breathed a sigh of relief. He had been as good as his word, he hadn't mentioned anything. But then she remembered his exact words of the encounter the previous night. "*It all depends,*" he had said, and that certainly did not mean never.

'Come on,' said Gloria, giving Naomi a little push, 'don't stand there like Lot's wife turned into a pillar of stone.'

'Salt,' corrected Naomi absentmindedly, 'it was salt, not stone.'

'Whatever it was, don't just stand there. We've got dear little Patrick to get organised, otherwise he'll end up doing precisely zilch as usual!'

Naomi laughed and followed Gloria down the corridor. Suddenly she felt more cheerful in spite of the niggling worry about the car, and how much it might cost. Luke hadn't spilt the beans, perhaps that was a good omen.

Gloria had decided to mount a campaign to get their locum senior house officer to do some work, rather than leave it to everyone else, and Naomi was more than willing to help. But their carefully laid plans were thwarted, however, as Luke had suddenly changed the rota and put him with Mr Sengupta in the referral clinic. It seemed he too had noticed Patrick's rather conspicuous absence in the department, and by putting him in the clinic under Mr Sengupta's watchful eye, there was no chance of him escaping.

'I'll be seeing any casualties that come in,' he said when he saw the two girls. 'Between us we should be able to keep things ticking over.'

Tick over the department certainly did that morning. A steady stream of minor accidents to begin with, then an RTA came in, blue light flashing as the ambulance sped silently to the emergency bay. They'd already had some warning over the radio telephone. 'Multiple injuries, patient in a bad way,' the ambulance driver had said. At the message, A and E swung into action, with a precision born of good training and plenty of practice.

'You come with me,' Luke instructed Naomi, and then turning to Gloria he'd said, 'Get Rose Murphy to retrieve young Patrick whatever his name is out of referral clinic. You'll need some extra help on this side.'

Without waiting to see if his instructions were followed, he started at a run towards the resuscitation room, Naomi following closely on his heels. They arrived just as the ambulance drew to a halt.

No time was wasted in words. Almost before the ambulance had stopped, the driver and mate were out, the double doors at the back flung open and the patient swiftly transferred, still on the stretcher, into the resus room.

They had not been exaggerating when they'd radioed that he was in a bad way. The patient, a man in his forties, most certainly had multiple injuries. In fact, looking at him as she set to work cutting away his clothing, Naomi wondered if there was any part of him that had not suffered damage in one way or another. The most obvious injuries were his badly crushed legs, and a deeply lacerated scalp wound, which extended down and through his left eye. Blood had soaked through every inch of his suit and underclothes, it was impossible to say for certain even what colour his hair might have been, as it too was matted with the brilliant crimson of fresh blood.

Naomi didn't worry about her clean uniform, all such niceties went out of the window in real emergencies. Both she and Luke became almost as bloody as their patient as they struggled to release the clothing.

'He's going to lose that eye, I'm afraid,' muttered Luke under his breath, as Naomi continued removing the clothing, and packed a collar around the patient's neck. She didn't need to be told to do it, knowing that it was always necessary to assume a spinal cord lesion until proved otherwise. All head and neck movements had to be kept to a minimum until the integrity of the cervical spine had been shown radiologically.

As soon as she had finished Luke started the urgent physical appraisal. The important thing was to make a rapid assessment. The fact that Luke was no theoretical doctor, but an extremely practical one with plenty of experience under his belt, soon showed.

'Cor,' she heard one of the ambulance men mutter in reverent tones, 'he's knows what he's about all right!'

Her sentiments exactly. She couldn't help but marvel at his expertise in dealing with multiple trauma. A less experienced doctor might well have looked at the bleeding, crushed legs, or the scalp laceration with the eye almost out of its socket, but Luke hardly glanced at that, but went straight to the chest. He had spotted immediately what Naomi knew many would perhaps have missed at first—a flailed chest. As he gently palpated the chest, his lean face was a mask of concentration.

'Paradoxical chest wall movement,' he muttered, glancing up briefly.

Naomi pulled down the oxygen mask from its place on the wall and turned on the piped oxygen supply. By now the rest of the resus team had arrived.

'Ventilate for apnoea, or respiratory inadequacy,' said Luke, 'keep the face mask on and aim to keep the arterial oxygen pressure above 10 k pa and the carbon dioxide below 5.5 k pa.' The anaesthetist took over from Naomi and followed Luke's instructions.

The next fifteen minutes were fifteen minutes of frantic activity, the whole team working with one thought in mind—to keep the patient breathing, to stop the bleeding and to replace the lost blood.

Luke and the anaesthetist cleared the airway of as much blood and vomit as possible by aspirating with a sucker, then inserted a cuffed endotracheal tube and connected the patient to the ventilator, already prepared by the technician. Naomi and the other nurse applied tourniquets as a temporary measure to stop the main areas of bleeding.

'Is he ready for theatre?' Luke asked briefly.

'Almost,' Naomi replied. 'The central venous pressure line is going in now.'

Luke didn't wait for the anaesthetist to finish, but picked up the phone from the side wall and punched out the extension number for theatre. They had already been alerted that a multiple trauma case would be coming.

'Mac? Oh, good, I'm glad it's you.' Mr McDonald was one of the County General's best surgeons. 'Our RTA is on his way up. Yes, yes, I'll organise an ophthalmic surgeon and an orthopaedic surgeon for later. But the stove-in chest is the greatest priority, in my opinion, and I think you'll agree.' Then the resus team heard him groan. 'Oh hell!' he exploded.

'Short of theatre nurses again?' the anaesthetist asked grimly.

'Too damned right.' Luke slammed the phone back into the wall cradle. Then suddenly he wheeled round to face Naomi. 'You've had theatre training, haven't you?'

'Yes, but . . .' Naomi raised her eyebrows in silent question.

'Good, you can go up and be an extra pair of hands. You don't mind, do you? I'll ring Theatre straight away and tell them they've got their extra nurse.' He reached out, squeezing her hands, smiling at her gratefully. There was no chance for her to say anything—anyway, words weren't needed. The patient needed immediate surgery. But even so, the clasp of his hands, and his smile, sent a warm thrill racing through Naomi. And she knew when he looked at her in that way, she'd have willingly jumped over the moon if he'd asked her to! Of course, so would anyone else, she told herself, it's all part of his irresistible charm!

Up in the trauma theatre, however, the outside world, including Luke, was forgotten by the operating team, as the lengthy and complex surgery proceeded. At long last the patient was finally stabilised. They'd done the best they could and Naomi, along with the rest of the team, felt exhausted but rewarded. It was challenging and very different from working in A and E, and she had enjoyed it.

But it was a long way past five o'clock, her normal off-duty time, before she staggered out of the operating theatre, having been on her feet all day. How she got through that evenings's waitressing she never knew, but somehow she did. Although several customers got scampi instead of steaks!

The rest of the week slid by in a blur of hard work. Naomi felt more and more tired and dispirited. It didn't help having the depressing fact hanging over her head that her car did need a new starter motor, and was too old for any garage to have one in stock. There was nothing for it but to use her feet, and cadge a lift every evening from Jim, the head waiter, who dropped her off at the end of her road. When Friday came, she had to catch the bus back to Longstone, a long and tiring journey, and by the time it eventually deposited her at the small village on the saltings, she was more than ready for her weekend break.

It wasn't until she was flopped out in the kitchen, relaying her tale of woe to Aunt Flo, that she remembered her promise to accompany Toby to the mill at Maltsworth with Bob and Janet.

Toby reminded her gleefully, 'You said you'd come. I want you to see the big boats too,' he added plaintively, seeing the reluctant expression cross her face. 'Oh, you must come!'

'Yes, I'm afraid you must,' said Aunt Flo firmly. 'Bob and Janet can't go—Janet has gone down with the 'flu.'

'Of course I will,' Naomi promised Toby, reassuring herself with the thought that at least Luke wouldn't be there.

She hadn't seen much of him for the rest of that week. Apart from calling her into his office to congratulate her on her theatre work, their contact and conversation had been minimal, which, Naomi firmly told herself, was just how it should be. The less she saw of him, the less chance there was that he'd bring up the subject of Toby's paternity again. The whole of the rest of the week had gone by without him mentioning either Toby or the restaurant; in fact by Friday Naomi was beginning to hope that he'd dismissed both topics from his mind. If he saw her with Toby again it would only refresh his memory. But as he wasn't going to be at the mill she had nothing to worry about. She could relax and enjoy the day.

The weekend flew past far too quickly for Naomi, and Sunday morning dawned bright and sunny. For Toby, however, Sunday couldn't come soon enough. He had talked of nothing else but power-boats the whole weekend, until she and Aunt Flo thought they'd be driven mad by his questions. Now that Sunday had actually arrived, he got up at the crack of dawn, and was dressed and ready to go practically before Naomi was even awake.

'Off you go, and have a lovely day,' said Aunt Flo, waving them off as they started the walk along the side of the saltings, towards the harbour at Maltsworth. 'You are lucky, I've always wanted to look over that tide mill.'

Naomi wished it was Aunt Flo going with Toby and not her, but said nothing. Now Sunday had arrived, she was feeling apprehensive again in case Luke did turn up after all. She hadn't confided to Aunt Flo about Luke and his unnervingly searching questions about Toby's father. Instinctively she felt the less said the better.

It was a beautiful calm day, a cloudless blue sky arching overhead, and only the faintest whisper of a breeze to disturb the sea grasses edging the path. Quite different from the previous Sunday with the force six wind that had been responsible for Toby's mishap, and the meeting with Luke. If only it hadn't been so windy that day, he would have remained in blissful ignorance of Toby's existence, and she wouldn't have been in the position of being pitied as an unmarried mother deserted by her lover. But what of it, she tried to reason sensibly, what did it matter what he thought? After this weekend and the next, she'd make quite certain that her life and Luke's ran in opposite directions once they were out of the hospital.

As they walked along the shoreline, they followed the ancient path, made by the passage of ponies' feet, in the days when they struggled along in the darkness, laden with smugglers' contraband. Normally Toby demanded to be told the story of the smugglers and their kegs of French brandy, but today power-boats occupied his mind to the exclusion of everything else. He raced ahead, Stubbs at his heels, the little dog frequently circling back to make sure Naomi was still following.

On arrival at the mill, Naomi lifted the heavy latch on the five-barred gate that sealed the mill

garden off from the shoreline path. At the sound
of the latch, two dalmations rushed out, barking
vociferously, but luckily for Stubbs, they proved to
be friendly. Matt appeared in the doorway and
waved at them to come on in.

'It's just me today, I'm afraid,' he said as soon
as they were within earshot. 'Janet's ill, as you
know, and Luke, who was intending to come, has
got held up on something.'

'Oh, what a pity, but we don't mind,' said
Naomi, trying to camouflage the surge of relief
that swept over her at his words. 'Anyway, Toby
will only have eyes for your boats. Engines take
precedence over human beings, I'm afraid, at the
moment.'

Matt laughed. 'A boy after my own heart,' he
said.

While Matt explained the intricacies of the
power-boats to Toby, Naomi contentedly
wandered around the enclosed garden. The brick
walls, mellowed by centuries of keeping out the sea
winds, glowed in the warm sunshine. The garden
was a riot of rambling roses and other old-
fashioned sweet-smelling flowers, a timeless,
relaxing place. The morning passed by in a haze of
warm sunshine, before they lunched, picnic
fashion, upstairs in the wheelhouse, the round
room at the top of the mill which had once served a
dual purpose as lighthouse and lookout.

'What did they look out for?' asked Toby.

'Customs men,' said Matt. 'The family that
owned this mill in olden days was the head of a

notorious smuggling gang. Many a dark deed was done here.'

That had settled it as far as Toby was concerned. They had to eat in the wheelhouse, no matter that it was as yet unfurnished. He was going to keep a lookout while he ate. Naomi protested, but Matt goodhumouredly let him have his own way.

'If you can't pretend to be a smuggler when you're little,' he said, 'when can you?'

There was no answer to that, so they lunched in the wheelhouse, Naomi and Matt having to make innumerable trips up and down the steep narrow steps that led to the little round room, carrying up all the food. Naomi could well understand the attraction it had for Toby, it was like being on top of the world, their little world. With glass for walls, they could see for miles in all directions. It was the perfect lookout.

While they ate, watching the tide roll in over the saltings, Toby bombarded Matt with questions, this time wanting stories of the smugglers. Matt obligingly thought up dreadfully gory stories to keep him happy.

When they had finished eating, Matt stood up and peered out. Where the mud of the saltings had been a few hours before was now a smooth expanse of water stretching as far as the eye could see. 'Time to take the boat out,' he said.

Toby jumped up, and was down the steps in the twinkling of an eye. 'I'm ready!' he called.

'Hang on, young man, we've got to clear up this lot.' Matt waved a hand in the direction of the remains of their picnic.

'No, you go on,' said Naomi. 'The tide is just right, and I'm not all that keen on the sea. I'll stay here and clear up these things.'

Matt protested, but not too vigorously, and Naomi could see he was as keen as Toby to get going, now that the draught of water was deep enough. 'I'll take good care of him,' he promised Naomi, disappearing down the steps after Toby. 'We'll be wearing a lifejacket, and a safety line.'

From her vantage point in the wheelhouse, Naomi watched them chug gently out from the boathouse, then the great red boat reared up from the water as Matt applied the throttle, and they roared away into the distance. She turned back and started clearing up. This was no easy matter, as she soon found out. Climbing down the precipitous steps with her arms full of crockery was difficult and hazardous, but slowly and surely she managed. At last, with everything cleared except the large tablecloth, she peered out from the wheelhouse for any sign of the boat returning. But there was not even the tiniest red dot to be seen on the horizon. They must have gone right over to the Island, she decided.

Gathering up the large tablecloth in her arms, she started down the steps, but the cloth was large and somehow one of the ends must have fallen, because halfway down, when there was nothing to hold on to, she stepped on a loose end and lost her balance. A little shriek escaped her lips, and frantically she tried to shed the tablecloth, vainly clutching wildly at the air. The next thing she knew she was being clasped against a rough sweater, held fast by a pair of strong arms.

'Arrived in the nick of time,' murmured Luke with a wry twist to his mouth.

'But Matt said you weren't coming,' Naomi gasped breathlessly.

'Just as well I changed my mind.'

'Er . . . yes, thank you.' Naomi tried to think clearly, tried to discount the wonderful, magical sensations racing through her body as she remained held close to his lean muscular frame. Was it her imagination, or was his heart racing as fast as her own? 'I'm all right now,' she tried to say coolly, putting her hands up against his chest, but somehow the words came out in a rush.

'I'm not sure I am,' came the husky response.

Intuitively she knew what he was about to do. She could have turned her head away, she could have tried to move, but she didn't. Instead she remained where she was, locked in his arms, her face turned up to his, ready to receive his kiss. She felt his whole frame shudder as he crushed her against him, and she lost her breath again as one arm encircled her waist, pulling her body intimately close, the other cupping the back of her head, as his lips came down on hers in a series of light, delicate kisses.

Her eyes closed, her slender fingers curling into the rough wool of his sweater, Naomi unashamedly drank in the nectar of his kisses. Sensing her willing acquiescence, Luke captured her mouth with his own, moving with a sensual, tantalising expertise, enticing a response Naomi was powerless to resist.

It seemed to her that the kiss went on and on for ever. The touch of his mouth was intoxicating, raising her sensual awareness to a peak she'd never known existed. Dart after dart of pleasure splintered through her body, and involuntarily melting against him, she gave herself up to this unknown pleasure.

For a brief second Luke broke away, but still held her close, gazing down at her with his slaty green eyes, now a turbulent as the Atlantic Ocean at the height of a storm. 'Naomi,' he groaned throatily, then his mouth claimed hers once more, this time with a bruising fierceness, his kisses growing in urgency as his breathing became harsher. His body pressed against hers demanded fulfilment.

'Naomi, Naomi!' Toby's voice, high-pitched with excitement, shattered the moment.

Cursing with the fluency and inventiveness of a born sailor, Luke turned away, running his fingers through his dark hair in a gesture of irritated frustration.

'Luke,' suddenly Naomi was desperate to explain, 'Toby and I, it's not like you th . . .' but she had left it too late, there was no time for explanations. Toby and Matt erupted into the room, like a couple of cannonballs, both talking at once, monopolising Luke's attention.

On the fringe of the conversation, Naomi took the opportunity of the chance to compose herself.

Swiftly raking her fingers through hair tousled by Luke's embrace, and praying her face wasn't too flushed, she gathered up the rather crumpled tablecloth. It had been completely forgotten in their brief moment of shared passion. Obliquely she studied Luke as he stood talking to Matt, and an involuntary shiver ran through her as she recalled the feel of that tall lean body against hers, a body that demanded total surrender. She touched her bruised lips, remembering the feel of the stern yet sensuous lips. Lips that had taken and possessed her whole being. Not that she had resisted in any way, she had been more than a willing captive to his mastery.

It was at that moment that Naomi knew she had fallen in love. The fact struck her with a sudden blinding force. She was hopelessly, helplessly, irrevocably in love with Luke Roderick, and knew she had to set the record straight as far as Toby was concerned. She had to tell him the truth, as far as she knew it. Even though common sense still told her that the chance of Luke actually feeling anything other than pure physical attraction was about as remote as the man in the moon.

She reminded herself sternly that the time he had shown most concern for her was when he thought she'd been wronged by another man. No doubt sorting out the problems of a damsel in distress appealed to the doctor in his make-up. But interpreting that into a more concrete and lasting form of caring was quite another matter! But she drew some comfort from the fact that she was sure

he had been as shattered as she had by their kiss.
What did it all mean?

As usual, her thoughts ran round and round in
ever decreasing circles, never reaching an answer.
Reluctantly Naomi was forced to conclude that as
she wasn't very good at interpreting her own
emotions, what good reason was there to suppose
she'd be any better at trying to fathom out what
Luke was really thinking?

All the same, she decided she would at least
make a move in the right direction, and tell Luke
the unvarnished truth concerning Toby's
parentage.

CHAPTER NINE

THE FATES, however, seemed to have other ideas in mind for Naomi as far as unburdening herself to Luke was concerned, because from the moment Matt and Toby arrived, there was never an opportunity to speak to Luke alone. Much as she loved Toby, and was fond of Matt, Naomi couldn't help wishing they'd disappear for five minutes. But Toby transferred his attention from Matt to Luke, and stuck to him like a limpet. There was no alternative but to console herself with the thought that at least she would have the chance to speak to him in private the following week when they were back at the hospital.

But to her frustration and exasperation, fate once again seemed to conspire against her, and it was not to be. When she checked in on duty the following Monday morning, there was no sign of Luke. Rose Murphy was in a very bad mood, and rushing about in a flap—or at least, rushing as fast as her size and weight would allow, complaining bitterly at the same time because Richard was late in returning from study leave.

'I know Patrick Rogers isn't much good,' she grumbled loudly when she spied Gloria and Naomi, 'but at least he's here, whereas Dr Nicholas . . .'

'Do I hear my name taken in vain?' called a cheery voice, as Richard skated round the corner. As usual he looked slightly dishevelled as he struggled into a newly laundered white coat, getting the sleeve tangled up with his stethoscope.

'You're late,' said Sister Murphy, glowering at him.

'I know, but I have some marvellous news.' Richard put his arms around her fat figure, and tried to lift her off her feet and give her a whirl, but gave up the unequal struggle and hugged her instead. 'You are now talking to Richard Nicholas, FRCS!'

'Oh,' Gloria squealed, 'well done, Richard!'

Naomi added her congratulations, and even Sister Murphy was pleased, although she said in a severe voice, 'Put me down, young man! Passing your exam is no reason for improper behaviour!'

'Ah, but Sister Murphy, you're *so* irresistible,' said Richard, giving her a final hug.

'Well, I do think that's going a bit overboard,' said Gloria when Sister Murphy had departed, pink-faced and flustered, into her office. 'Irresistible indeed!'

Richard grinned, and wagged an admonishing finger. 'Just watch what you're saying, Nurse. You're speaking to the boss. I'm in charge this week. Patrick Rogers is staying on as a locum, and we've got a new senior house officer, David Chan.'

As he spoke a diminutive young Chinese man, as neat and tidy as Richard was untidy, rounded the corner and joined them. When the introductions were completed, Naomi took the chance to ask casually the question that had been hovering on her lips from the moment Richard had said he was in charge.

'Where is Luke Roderick?'

'Gone to London. The Royal College of Surgeons.'

'But he didn't . . .'

'Say anything? Richard interrupted. 'No, he couldn't. Apparently he didn't even know himself until last night. He rang me at home, and told me I would be in charge for this side of casualty, with Mr Sengupta to refer to, of course.'

'But what's he doing up in London?' Gloria was curious too.

'There's a big scientific meeting all this week, and one of the main speakers has dropped out through illness. They wanted a well-known personality, so who better than star of stage, screen and the County General A and E department, Mr Luke Roderick— boom, boom!' Richard struck a theatrical pose.

'His fame has caught up with him at last,' joked Naomi, trying to ignore the bitter feeling of disappointment that swept over her.

'Never left him,' Richard replied with a grin.

Naomi bit her lip in vexation. She had steeled herself to blurt out the truth of Toby's origins the very moment she set eyes on Luke. And now she'd just found out he wasn't going to be anywhere near her for a whole week. And in a week he'll have forgotten all about that kiss, so there'll be no point in unburdening your soul! The nasty little voice, always ready to pop up and distract her, taunted cruelly from the back of her mind. Oh, shut up, thought

Naomi fiercely, wishing her subconscious could be more reassuring, and tell her that Luke would be waiting with bated breath for the next moment he could set eyes on her! But it seemed that the plain, practical common sense that had always stood her in such good stead most of her life was now determined to pour cold water on any romantic notions she might be harbouring. Forget Luke Roderick, and get on with your own life! But even though she could give herself such good advice, Naomi knew the chances of her being able to follow it were practically nil.

'Come on, don't just stand there, this morning's customers are waiting,' Gloria's voice interrupted her morose reflections.

Naomi jumped. 'Oh yes,' she stammered, hastily collecting her scattered thoughts, 'let's go.' She hurried down the corridor towards the reception area.

Gloria caught up with her at the desk. 'Are you all right?' she asked curiously, staring hard at her as they both picked up a pile of notes.

'Of course—why?' With an effort Naomi forced her voice to sound casually light.

Gloria, however, was not to be deterred. 'I thought you looked rather worried.'

'You've got an over-active imagination,' said Naomi, firmly harnessing her wandering thoughts and determinedly pushing Luke Roderick to the back of her mind, 'that's your problem, Gloria.'

'Yes,' agreed Gloria, 'I suppose I have.' She giggled suddenly. 'It's certainly working overtime when I think of Luke Roderick up in London, with all those gorgeous women!' Naomi looked surprised and Gloria warmed to her theme. 'Well, it's human nature, isn't it? He's bound to go and look up all those people he worked with on TV. Oh, I wish I was in London and not here,' she added.

'Yes, I suppose he will,' answered Naomi slowly. It was not something she had thought about herself, but now that Gloria had mentioned it, she supposed it was pretty obvious. Of course Luke must have many friends and acquaintances in the show business world.

'We don't stand a chance, said Gloria with an exaggerated sigh, 'two little backwoods nurses—he'll never look at us.'

'I'm not a backwoods nurse,' said Naomi. 'Speak for yourself! Anyway,' she added, 'I don't particularly want him to look at me! I can't think what you see in him, he's nothing special. Sometimes I think all the women in this hospital have gone stark raving mad, and just because he's been on TV.'

'It's not just that. He's a fascinating man,' said Gloria dreamily, 'you can't deny that. Mr Gilbert!' she called, suddenly switching back to her efficient nurse voice.

The chance for a reply was lost as the patient in question got up and hobbled over. Not that Naomi could think of a truthful one. But the fact that it was true that every woman who met Luke found him fascinating merely reinforced her previous gloomy thoughts. It stood to reason that a man like Luke would hardly be likely to bother to give her a second thought. A plain ordinary staff nurse, and one with, as he thought, an illegitimate son to boot! No, she had to face the unpalatable truth, that he'd merely taken advantage of the fact that she'd literally fallen straight into his arms the previous afternoon. Probably most other men would have done the same, she told herself firmly. All the same, she couldn't prevent her heart doing a triple somersault at the memory. She had never dreamed, not in her wildest flights of fantasy, that any man could suddenly have her floundering in such deep emotional waters. Uncharted territory as far as Naomi was concerned, dark and rather frightening. She had fallen in love much too quickly, and much too easily; and she had to acknowledge that Luke had not given her the slightest indication that he was interested in her in a romantic way.

He had kissed her passionately, it was true, but now that she thought about it, he hadn't seemed unduly perturbed when they'd been disturbed, apart from his initial reaction. In fact, when she came to analyse it more clearly, she realised he hadn't even glanced at her again that afternoon.

Her thoughts wandered back to Toby. Perhaps if she could explain . . . if, if, if . . . She sighed, and tried to compose her thoughts once more. There was no point in worrying, life would work itself out, as Aunt Flo was so fond of saying. But how could it, when the man she loved almost certainly thought of her as a girl who had hopped in and out of bed so many times she didn't even know who the father of her own child was! Hardly an ideal way to begin any relationship! No, Aunt Flo's little homily would never work if she couldn't put that fact straight.

'Elaine Jackson,' she called the name of the first patient from her pile of notes. Work—that was the answer, it was the only remedy she knew to help her forget her problems. Maybe with luck it might even take her mind off the wretched man himself.

Thoughts of Luke, however, certainly did disappear in a flash when Elaine Jackson and her mother came forward at Naomi's call. There was something about the way the child hung back, unwilling it seemed even to take her mother's hand. Intuitive warning bells sounded in Naomi's head. This wasn't a straightforward casualty case, she was sure of that.

Smiling encouragingly, she went forward and took the small girl's hand in hers. 'Now what's the problem?' she asked, leading mother and daughter towards a cubicle and pulling the curtains close.

The child maintained a sullen silence. Glancing down at the admission chart, Naomi saw that she was eleven years old, although she was small and looked much younger.

'She had a fall and hurt her arm,' said her mother.

'I'll just have a look,' said Naomi gently, carefully removing the child's cardigan, 'and then we'll call the doctor.'

She noted how the child flinched as soon as she touched her, as if more than just her arm hurt, but she said nothing. As soon as the painfully thin little arm was exposed, however, Naomi knew why the warning bells had been sounding. It was no accidental injury she was examining. The child's arm had been wrung by someone with a strong hand, the marks of the fingers were plain to see.

'Any other injuries from the fall?' She asked the question casually, not wanting to alert the mother to her suspicions.

'No, no, none at all.' The answer came back in a flash, much too fast and pat.

'I think I'll take Elaine along to X-Ray now,' said Naomi firmly, 'if you would like to wait here, Mrs Jackson.'

'But I . . .' the child's mother made a movement as if to stop her.

'We'll only be a few minutes.' Naomi whipped Elaine out of the cubicle and away before Mrs Jackson had a chance to object. The child needed to be examined, and if possible questioned, without the mother being present.

She hurried down the corridor, and grabbed Richard, who happened to be passing. 'Child abuse, I think,' she said under her breath, nodding towards Elaine at her side.

'Oh God, I wish Luke was here,' said Richard, looking at Elaine.

'So do I,' echoed Naomi, but this time her personal desires had been forgotten, she was thinking of Elaine. Luke was so good with children, they could have used his compassion and insight with this case.

At the end of the day it was a chastened and unhappy Naomi who trudged off to work at the Water's Edge. She had wanted work to help her forget Luke, but not the sort of case they'd had that day. Her eyes filled with tears as she remembered Elaine's poor bruised and battered little body. No wonder she'd flinched when Naomi had first taken off her cardigan, and how the mother could have sat there, knowing and yet lying, was something Naomi could not understand. But worse was to follow. Richard had called down a paediatrician who dealt with child abuse, and she had found after a physical examination of Elaine that not only had she been beaten, but that she had been sexually abused as well by her stepfather. After questioning, it had transpired that everything had happened with the knowledge of the mother. Naomi shuddered. Such evil repulsed her, it was beyond the comprehension of ordinary people. She was glad she didn't deal with cases such as that every day. Broken bones and bodies she could cope with, but not that.

The aftermath of the case hung over A and E for the rest of the week. Both Naomi and Richard had to give comprehensive statements to the police, as it was now in their hands, and when Friday evening came and she started the journey back to Longstone she was heartily glad to say goodbye to that particular week.

After a decent interval of allowing her to kiss his grubby cheek, Toby wriggled free. 'Motor racing on Sunday,' he announced, jumping up and down in barely contained excitement.

'Oh!' Naomi stopped dead, she had completely forgotten. 'But, Toby, I don't have a car——' she began.

'Matt's taking us,' said Toby matter-of-factly. He had obviously discussed the plans at length. 'He came round this week and told me. 'We've got to be ready by eight o'clock Sunday morning. It's a long way to Siverstone.' He gabbled out the information, his mind already running on ahead to their day out.

'Did he say whether Luke was coming with us?' Naomi tried to sound casual as she posed the question to Aunt Flo, whose mind was also running on ahead, busily planning the picnic food they would need to take.

She reeled off a list of goodies she aimed to prepare for the picnic, but stopped mid-sentence at Naomi's question. 'Who, dear?' she asked vaguely.

'Luke—Luke Roderick. You remember, the man who fished Toby out of the Solent.'

'Oh, that doctor you work with. Well, dear, why didn't you ask him? Because I certainly don't know, and Matt didn't mention anyone else when he came round.'

'Luke has been in London all week,' said Naomi. 'I haven't seen him, so I don't know.'

'You're hoping he's coming.' Aunt Flo stopped thinking about food and gave Naomi her full attention. Then she beamed, her grey head nodding in approval as she said, 'Good. It's about time you started looking at young men, and I must say, from what I've heard from Toby, he does sound very nice.'

'I'm not interested in Luke as a *man*,' muttered Naomi hastily. Aunt Flo was much too quick at cottoning on to things she didn't want her to. 'I was just wondering whether or not he was coming.'

'Well, I'll put in an extra pork pie in case, and another two cans of beer. There,' Aunt Flo waved the list at Naomi, 'I think that'll do you for Sunday.'

Naomi took the proffered piece of paper, anxious to get her aunt's mind off the subject of Luke. After reading it, she burst out laughing and handed the list back. 'We're going out for a day to Silverstone,' she said, 'not a two-month expedition to the North Pole.'

'I wouldn't like you to run short of anything,' said Aunt Flo, who believed in keeping a well stocked larder. The list was put away, and the subject of Luke forgotten; although not by Naomi.

Sunday morning dawned wet and drizzly, but with the promise of fine weather to come. Matt turned up on time and loaded the laden picnic basket into the boot. 'What's in here?' he puffed as he staggered under the weight. 'Are we feeding an entire racing team?'

Naomi laughed. 'Very probably,' she said.

The journey to Silverstone was faster than she thought, and she was quite happy to relax and sit back and watch the countryside slide past the windows of Matt's hugely luxurious car. He hadn't mentioned Luke, so neither had she. Obviously he wasn't going to be there. Although it was strange, because she could have sworn on the day that she and Toby had nearly drowned, Luke had said he *was* going to Silverstone.

'Ever been to a Grand Prix?' asked Matt.

'Never,' answered Naomi truthfully, 'but this isn't

the Grand Prix, is it, not today?'

'My dear girl, don't you ever read the newspapers? Of course it is,' chuckled Matt.

A ripple of disquiet fluttered in the pit of Naomi's stomach. A Grand Prix! Dirk Roderigues would be there. Don't start being ridiculous, she told herself sternly. Even if he is, he's hardly likely to notice you amongst the thousands of spectators, particularly as he'll be passing you at about a hundred and seventy mph! She settled back. How silly she was! Lately her imagination had the nasty habit of running riot over every little thing concerning Toby.

When they arrived the sun was blazing down, and to Naomi's suprise Matt put a sticker on the car and was waved through by the race officials. They drove past all the crowds queueing up to get into the car parks adjoining the race track, straight into the enclosure itself. Toby was nearly bursting with excitement as Matt drew up beside a flamboyantly coloured caravan; the colours were sickenly familiar to Naomi's eyes.

'Headquarters of the Ragazzi Team,' Matt announced as they climbed out.

Naomi's heart had almost stopped before he had spoken—he didn't need to tell her. She recognised the colours at once. The Ragazzi Team was Dirk Roderigues' team. For one frantic moment she contemplated grabbing Toby and making a run for it, but too late, Luke appeared from nowhere and descended upon them. He took Toby's hand and started leading them towards the pits.

Naomi followed anxiously. The smell of the fuel

and the heat was overpowering, and she felt sick with apprehension. Luke turned and reprimanded her. 'Come on, Naomi, stop dawdling. I promised Toby could meet my brother before the race started, and we've only got a few minutes.'

His brother! At his words, wave upon wave of relief flooded over her, and she hurried after their rapidly disappearing figures. Everything was going to be all right. Of course she should have realised, Dirk Roderigues would already be in his car. They were going to meet Luke's brother. Perhaps he worked for TV—yes, it all made sense, that was quite possible.

She lost sight of them for a moment, their figures swallowed up in the milling crowd of mechanics in dark blue overalls, TV cameras and cameramen. But then she found them. She had no difficulty in spotting Luke and Toby, they were standing beside the distinctively coloured Ragazzi Team car.

Some of the cars were already revving, ready to go out on the grid. She saw Luke put his arm around the driver who was standing beside the car, and then they turned round towards her. It all happened in a split second. The driver, helmet in hand, looked down at Toby and then straight across at her. It was Dirk Roderigues. Naomi felt her face blanch as she saw Toby and Dirk together. There was not the faintest shadow of doubt in her mind now about Toby's father. Toby was a small replica of the man he stood gazing up at so adoringly—his hero, Dirk Roderigues, the racing driver.

'Naomi!' Dirk's voice sounded hoarse, but even so it cut across the screaming engines of the other cars in the pits. Then he looked down at Toby again, and back to her, and she knew he had guessed.

'Dirk, I . . .' She started forward, but Luke was suddenly beside her, his hand restraining her.

'Whatever it is, it will have to wait,' he said harshly. They're almost under starter's orders.'

In a daze she let Luke hold her back, while the team manager pulled the fireproof mask over Dirk's face and then clamped the heavy crash helmet in place. Her last sight was of his dark eyes looking at Toby, then with a roar the car disappeared from the pit in a haze of blue fumes, out into the dazzling sunshine of the track.

'Isn't it exciting!' Toby shrieked, dragging her forward.

'Yes,' said Naomi, desperately stretching her lips into what she hoped resembled a smile.

'Isn't it?' said Luke, looking at Naomi with eyes so cold she felt that the blood must surely freeze in her veins. 'I always knew there was more to you than met the eye, but never this. Not this!'

'But . . .' Now was the time, she had to tell him about Tiffany.

'Come on, what the hell are you doing standing here? We'll miss the start.' Matt grasped Naomi's arm and Toby's hand, and led the way into the grandstand.

She was vaguely conscious of Luke remaining behind, standing quite still, and muttering something to Matt before she was dragged off. Her mind was in turmoil. How could Dirk Roderigues be Luke's brother? But he was, and that was why she had seen the likeness between Luke and Toby.

She had to find out. She managed to gasp the question to Matt as they squeezed their way past the spectators crowded into the grandstand.

'What?' Matt wasn't paying her attention, his concentration being focused on the grid, where the cars were lined up like a pack of snarling tigers straining at the leash.

She repeated her question, and it registered this time. 'Oh,' Matt turned briefly and grinned, oblivious to the panic in her voice, 'Dirk Roderigues isn't his real name, of course, it's his racing name. He thinks it's more exciting than Derek Roderick.'

Naomi missed the spectacular beginning of the race, she was craning her head to look at Luke, who was standing with the team mechanics. His hands were thrust deep into the pockets of his jeans, and his face was as black as thunder. It was only after the first lap that she began to pay attention to the race, and became conscious that Matt was swearing softly.

'Bloody fool,' she heard him mutter, and then, 'What the hell does he think he's playing at?'

'What's the matter?' She turned to watch the race, just in time to see a red and yellow flash, a puff of blue as tyres burned on the track, and Dirk hurled the car through the corner.

'If he drives like that he'll never survive the race!'

'Like what?' asked Naomi. Never having seen motor racing before, she thought all cars cornered the way Dirk had just done.

'Like a madman. He's cutting the corners much too fine, and not changing down through the gears until the very last moment. It's almost as if he's not thinking of what he's doing.'

The words were no sooner out of Matt's mouth than the race commentator's voice echoed over the loudspeaker system. 'There's been a crash, someone is out of the race. I think it's Dirk Roderigues—yes, it is. The car's on fire, they're trying to get him out. Oh, my God, this is a bad one!'

With a muttered oath, Matt leaped up and started scrambling out of the stand. Blindly Naomi followed, and pulling Toby with her pushed and stumbled past the solid mass of spectators until they too had reached the pits, where Matt was in urgent conversation with Luke.

She joined the fringe of the group of mechanics and officials surrounding Matt and Luke. Her eyes caught Luke's gaze, and in one stride he was over to her side.

'He crashed because he wasn't thinking of his driving.' His voice was low, so that no one else would overhear, but Naomi shrank back at the cold despairing rage in every word. 'He was thinking of you—you and his son. If Dirk dies, it will be your fault!'

With that he was gone, leaving Naomi and Toby standing alone and forlorn amidst the frantic chaos around them.

CHAPTER TEN

THE REST of that afternoon passed in a confused haze of unadulterated misery. Naomi was vaguely conscious of holding a bewildered Toby's hand and following Matt everywhere, mainly because she was at a loss as to what to do next. There didn't seem to be anything else she could do. Silently standing by Matt's side, she watched as Dirk's unconscious form, swathed in sterile wraps, was loaded carefully into an ambulance, a saline drip rattling along beside him, and an oxygen mask clamped to his face.

Their last glimpse was of a grim-faced Luke at his brother's side as the doors closed. Then the ambulance roared away, siren screaming, as it cut an impatient swathe through the inquisitive crowds.

Still following Matt, Naomi and Toby went with him back to the Ragazzi Team caravan. No one was talking much, and a heavy depressing atmosphere prevailed. the crash had affected everyone but there was nothing anyone could do except sit around and wait for news. Naomi prayed silently that Dirk's injuries wouldn't be too serious, that she'd be able to do what she should have done years ago, unite him with his son. Only now did she truly realise, with painful clarity, that whatever her own feelings, she owed it to both of them, and she ought to have made an effort and contacted Dirk right at the very beginning. But all she could do now was to hope that she hadn't left it too late. Luke's accusing words echoed round and round inside her head, until she felt like screaming. *'If he dies it will be your fault.'*

The news, when it came over the radio telephone in the caravan was bad, but could have been worse. Luke spoke to the team manager, and then to Matt. Dirk was burned, but not too badly, he had two fractured legs and a fractured arm, but the most worrying thing was that he had not recovered consciousness, and he was about to go to X-Ray for a brain scan.

After the news bulletin, everyone packed up quietly and went their separate ways. There was no point in hanging around any longer. Matt took Naomi and Toby back to Longstone. It was a long and silent journey. Naomi unpacked Aung Flo's hamper, but neither she nor Matt could touch anything, only Toby ate, and even his ravenous appetite was diminished.

When they arrived at the cottage, Matt helped them from the car. Naomi hesitated, awkwardly searching for something to say. Toby clung on to her, his little face grave and worried.

Matt found the words. He took Toby's solemn face between his hands and smiled. 'It's a risk all drivers take, Toby. Dirk knew that before he started out today, he always knows. But he never stops driving.' He ruffled Toby's hair. 'You wait and see, it won't be long before he's back behind the wheel of a formula one car again, and next time we go to watch, we'll give him strict instructions not to crash.'

Toby smiled hesitantly. 'He's not going to die, then?'

'Good heavens, no,' said Matt heartily. 'Whatever gave you that idea?' But his eyes, as he glanced across at Naomi, gave the lie to his bluff cheerfulness. She knew he was worried sick, just as she was.

Naomi went through the following Monday in A and E dealing with the cases that came before her with an automatic precision. She wasn't aware of making any conscious decisions, she functioned on autopilot, even to the extent of joining halfheartedly in the usual banter of the department.

Luke wouldn't be there, Sister Murphy told them importantly. He'd telephoned to tell her that his brother had been involved in a motor racing accident, and that he was staying at the hospital with him.

'Fancy that,' said Richard when she'd gone. 'Sinbad the Surgeon's brother is Dirk Roderigues the racing driver, and to think we didn't know!'

'Why should you?' said Naomi quietly. 'The name is different.'

'Heavens, what a lark,' said Gloria, 'two famous brothers! I hope he brings Dirk here, I've always thought he was gorgeous.'

'If he survives,' said Naomi. 'He's still in a coma.'

'How come you know so much about it?' queried Richard curiously.

'Oh, I . . . er . . . heard it on the news.' lied Naomi hastily, hurrying back to her tasks before any more awkward questions could be asked.

After work at the restaurant that night, she trudged back to her bed-sit as usual. In the dark shadows of the overhanging trees, everything seemed to close in on her, and Luke's words rang with renewed intensity through her head. *'It will be your fault, your fault, your fault.'* Every footstep repeated the words, and every word turned like a knife inside of her, until the pain became unbearable.

Mercifully, exhaustion overtook her the moment she climbed into bed, and she fell into a deep and dreamless sleep. The early morning sun awoke her long before the alarm went off, and she lay for a few moments savouring the peace and quiet with pleasure, although a vague uneasiness lurked at the back of her mind. Suddenly she sat bolt upright in bed, as the uneasiness took concrete form. Everything flooded back. Dirk Roderigues was Luke's brother. The accident—would he have regained consciousness? Stubbornly determined, she never even allowed herself to think of any other possibilities, other than that he would recover, as she hurried through the morning routine of preparing for work. Luke was in his office when she arrived.

'How is his brother?' she whispered hastily to Rose Murphy as she reported for duty.

'Still unconscious, although apparently they can't

find anything wrong on the scan.' Sister looked selfrighteously serious. 'Luke's obviously beside himself with worry,' she said 'so I think we all ought to do what we can to make life easier for him.'

'Of course we will,' said Gloria, joining them, 'although work might help to take his mind off it.'

'Yes, I think he probably feels that too.' Sister Murphy nodded towards Naomi. 'He's going to do the referral clinic this morning, so could you go and collect the notes? It is your turn for the clinic, isn't it?'

'Yes,' replied Naomi with a sinking heart. Why did it have to be her? She'd have done anything to have kept out of the way until Dirk recovered. *'If he recovers,'* the voice at the back of her subconscious suddenly said.

She collected the notes from Paula, pausing as usual to have a word with the chatty receptionist. She was always glad of an opportunity to gossip, although all she wanted to talk about that morning was Luke and his famous brother Dirk Roderigues—not a subject Naomi was keen to expand upon. Then Richard nabbed her and asked her if she was feeling all right.

'You look awfully peaky still,' he observed, his keen eyes noting her drawn face, the golden-brown eyes enormous in the pallor of her face. 'Are you sure you're not sickening for something?'

'You're the doctor,' said Naomi, making a feeble attempt at a joke. 'What do you prescribe for the result of a night on the tiles?' However, she had the feeling she hadn't fooled Richard one iota, because he didn't answer, but gave her a strangely quizzical look before she started off in the direction of Luke's office.

Once in the office, the questions she longed to ask about Dirk's condition died in her throat. Luke's expression strangled them at birth. Instead she gulped, and ended up saying lamely. 'The referral notes,' as she laid them carefully on the side of the desk where they were always kept.

'I suppose it's too much to expect you to ask how your one-time lover is?' Luke said quietly. Naomi gave an involuntary shiver, soft menace was in the very timbre of his voice.

'Dirk wasn't . . .' she began hastily.

'Oh no, of course not, I'd forgotten. You don't know who Toby's father is, do you! So many men in your life that you can't remember. So why should you bother to remember Dirk? Well, I'll tell you one thing—' rising he crossed to Naomi. 'My brother remembered you well enough, and it's because of you he crashed.' He gave a mirthless laugh. 'On account of a worthless woman who didn't care enough about him to acknowledge him as the father of her child.'

It was the contemptuous tone of voice that did it. Without thinking Naomi raised her hand and brought it down with a stinging force across the angle of Luke's jaw. A telltale red stain spread across the lower half of his face, the exact imprint of the shape of her hand.

'Why, you little . . .! he reached out angrily towards her.

Naomi backed away. 'Don't you dare touch me, don't even speak to me,' she half sobbed, half hissed. 'I don't owe you any explanations, and I don't have to listen to your insults!'

Fury engulfed her. His words defiled Tiffany. Silly and headstrong her sister might have been, but she hadn't slept around, of that Naomi was certain. But Luke's precious brother Dirk, what had he done? Nothing, nothing at all to find out what had happened to Tiffany. If he had done something, he would have known years ago that he was the father to a son, and that Tiffany had died giving birth. But he hadn't cared enough to make even one enquiry. Her own failure to contact Dirk suddenly seemed to pall into insignificance besides Dirk's lack of concern.

The angry words came spilling out without thought. 'Your brother is purer than the driven snow, I suppose! I read the newspapers. How many girlfriends has he had? I doubt if he can keep count! I'm sorry he's crashed and is injured, but that doesn't give you the right to start jumping to conclusions. Men are all the same—self righteous! Why is it everything *he* did is all right, whereas anything you think *I* did is wrong?'

Without waiting for an answer she flew out of the office, slamming the door behind her with a crash that resounded up and down the corridor. Gloria and Richard, standing by the reception desk, looked up in surprise at the noise.

'You'll have to do the clinic, Gloria,' said Naomi 'and *please do not ask me to explain!*'

Although not one of the world's most tactful creatures, even Gloria could see that Naomi had really meant every word she said. Raising her eyebrows expressively to Richard, she silently entered Luke's office. Luckily Sister Murphy had gone off to a nursing officers' meeting, so she didn't notice the change in her rota system, and no explanatioons were necessary.

Afterwards Gloria reported to a mystified Richard that Luke hadn't queried her appearance either. 'I don't know what happened between him and Naomi, but he was in one hell of a mood. Luckily I didn't do anything wrong. If I had, I think he might well have strangled me with his bare hands!'

Richard pulled a face. 'Naomi was pretty strange too,' he said 'near to tears most of the time, if you ask me.'

It was true, Naomi had felt near to tears—tears of rage mixed with sorrow. Anger that Luke should have jumped to the conclusion that she was a slut. True, he hadn't actually used that word, but he'd implied it nevertheless. She'd never been particularly feminist in her views before, but now she felt vehemently angry. The injustice hurt. What right had he to assume his brother had been wronged? He knew nothing of the facts; he was adopting a typically male chauvinist attitude.

It was different not so long ago, she thought scornfully. His tender concern for her, wanting the father to acknowledge paternity. She had been a poor wronged girl then. But as with so many men before him, it was all different now he knew his brother was

the father. Now that it touched his own life she had
suddenly became Jezebel the temptress, the woman
who had led his poor little innocent brother astray.
Poor little innocent brother be damned! she fumed.

All the same, she wished she hadn't exploded, but
had kept her head, instead of blowing her top. Then
she could have told him how Tiffany had died alone
and unloved by the man who had made her pregnant.
That it was his brother Dirk who was the heartless
one—because if he had been in the slightest bit caring,
he would have been with Tiffany, or at least given her
son some financial support. But he had chosen to
ignore her. It was the age-old story, thought Naomi
scornfully, of a man discarding a woman when he had
grown tired of her. Luke was probably the same. All
those stories in the papers about a different woman in
every port when he'd been doing the voyage for
TV—she snorted angrily at the mere thought. Both
brothers were tarred with the same brush. She and
Toby were better off without them.

It was anger that kept her going through the rest of
the day, and then through another exhausting spell at
the Water's Edge. The enforced walk to work had
helped soothe some of her anger, and calm her
jagged nerves a little. But it was only a little. For in
spite of her anger, she couldn't blot out the tender
incredulous look that had flashed across Dirk's face
as he had looked at Toby. It wasn't the look of a
hard-hearted man, much as she wanted to believe
that he was. Dirk's face continually floated before
her eyes, tying her heart up in a tight knot of pain.

'My goodness, ducks, you look all in!' Molly

solicitous as ever, fussed around her, and ushered her firmly into a chair in the kitchen. 'Now you sit down there, and have this bit of steak and salad.'

'Steak?' Naomi looked at it doubtfully. The staff didn't usually get steak.

'A spare piece, said Molly firmly. 'Eat it up before the others come in.'

Naomi grinned for the first time that day. Molly was incorrigible, her motherly spoiling did Naomi a power of good, and before she knew it she began spilling out the whole story, right from the very beginning with Toby's birth in the remote Welsh hospital.

Molly listened in silence and then said, 'Well, love, you know what you've got to do, don't you?'

'I suppose so,' said Naomi, knowing and yet dreading the task ahead. Now that she was calmer she knew she had to tell Luke the truth whether Dirk lived or died. But what she dreaded most was his certain anger at the way she had kept Toby's birth undisclosed from his blood relations. There were other problems too that had to be faced, Toby had a whole host of other relations. The cosy little world they had shared, just the three of them, would disappear for ever. She felt an aching empty void at the mere thought, but the truth had to be told. Molly had merely confirmed what in her heart of hearts she had known all along.

'Thanks, Jim, Naomi slammed the car door shut

and waved to the head waiter as he drove off into the night, leaving her the long walk along the darkened street, back to her digs.

Immersed in thought as she was, trying to sort out the shambles of her mind, the steady footsteps a few yards behind her passed unnoticed. Normally in a hurry, that night she walked slowly, easy prey for the man behind her. Without warning a hand grabbed her shoulder violently, snapping her head back with a jerk. His other hand started fumbling roughly with the buttons on the front of her blouse.

The man was huge, she could tell that by the strength of his arms, and by the weight of his body as he dragged her against him. His breath was foul, reeking of alcohol, and he was uttering coarse animal-like grunts as he struggled to push her to the ground.

I mustn't panic, I must scream, attract attention, I mustn't panic—the thoughts drummed through her brain, as she tried to remember what they'd been taught at self-defence classes. She opened her mouth and tried to scream, but nothing came from her paralysed throat. The buttons at the front of her blouse flew off, spraying in all directions, and a loathsome hand pushed inside her bra.

Filled with revulsion at the assailant's grasping touch, Naomi felt her brain suddenly click into action. She screamed loud and long, at the same time kicking backwards, glad for once that she had on the high-heeled shoes that caused her so much discomfort. She felt the sharpness of the heel grate against his kneecap, and he growled in pain. Good, she'd hurt him—she kicked again, even harder this time, and the pain made him slacken his grip just a little; but it was enough. It gave Naomi the chance to break away and start running.

The house had never seemed so far away. She ran, unaware that she was screaming all the way. Stumbling over the uneven paving stones in her haste, she could hear the man lumbering after her. He was gaining on her with his longer legs, and without high heels to slow him down. Before they had been an advantage, now they were a hindrance, but there was not time to stop and take off her shoes.

Oh, please, please let someone hear me! she prayed, her breath coming in painful choking gasps—and then, as if answer to her silent prayer, the front door of her landlady's house opened, and the light from the hall streamed out into the night. A large man stood silhouetted in the doorway. Naomi's heart gave a great leap of relief. There was no mistaking the outline of that figure.

'Luke!' she heard her voice scream his name as if from very far away.

His tall figure moved swiftly forward into the darkness. Like a panther he leapt at her assailant, felling him in one swift blow. Then, turning, he gathered a sobbing Naomi into his arms.

'Hush, hush,' he whispered, cradling her trembling body close, stroking her hair gently, 'it's all over now.'

Naomi clung to him, vaguely aware that the man who had attacked her had scrambled up with a muttered oath and was retreating. The sound of his running footsteps receded into the distance. Great hiccuping sobs threatened to engulf her as raising her head she tried to speak, but Luke merely whispered, 'Shush' and held her closer.

Burying her face against the warmth of his chest, and listening to the comforting steady beat of his heart, she gradually quietened her sobs. Everything about Luke exuded a comforting strength. If only she could stay in the safe haven of his arms for ever and ever!

If only Luke could always be there; those were her last coherent thoughts before she fell asleep. Luke had dealt with everything—a hysterical landlady, the police—and had finally insisted on Naomi taking a sleeping tablet. She hadn't demurred, having someone take charge was such a relief, and even more of a relief was the fact that he'd told her Dirk was out of danger and she mustn't worry.

He smiled lopsidedly as he tucked her into bed and said. 'Don't worry, Naomi, everything will turn out just fine for you, you'll see.'

'But, Luke . . .' She knew she had something to tell him, something important, but in her confused state she couldn't remember what it was.

'Hush!' Placing a finger on her lips, Luke had quietened her. 'It will all come out in the wash, wait and see.'

Naomi smiled at him sleepily. He had used one of Aunt Flo's favourite expressions, and she felt strangely comforted.

As she drifted off into unconsciousness, the edges of her mind blurred by the effect of the sleeping pill, she could have sworn that Luke had bent and kissed her gently on the mouth before he left the room. Or was it a dream?

CHAPTER ELEVEN

NAOMI lay quietly for a few moments, watching the golden shaft of sunlight slanting across the floor of her bedroom. A sense of well being lay in a languorous mantle over her, until the memory of the previous night gradually began creeping back into her consciousness.

She sat up at the memory. Luke had been her saviour last night, but today no one could save her from what she knew she must do. She must go and see Dirk, and tell him the truth about Tiffany and Toby, the boy she had brought up as if he were her own son. The worst thing would be admitting that she had suspected all along that Dirk had been the father, and that for her own selfish reasons she had remained silent. The knowledge of that hurt her. It was the first time she had ever openly and honestly admitted it to herself, and the brutal truth was painful.

Slowly she showered and dressed, and when Luke's powerful car drew up outside the house she was ready. No formal arrangements had been made the previous night, at least none that she could remember, but she had known without having to be told that he would come.

Watching his tall figure with the distinctive loping stride coming up the garden path, she reached up and touched her lips, allowing herself a brief moment of luxury, wondering whether or not his lips really had touched hers fleetingly the night before, or whether it had been a figment of her imagination. He had been tender and gentle then, but she still suspected he would be angry when he knew she had deliberately kept the truth from his brother. She had already encountered the lash of his anger, and wasn't anxious to experience it again. Escape, however, was impossible. The moment had come to face him and his brother Dirk.

Feeling acutely nervous, Naomi slowly descended the staircase into the hall. She wished she could think of something to say, something cheerful and matter-of-fact. Anything to shatter the brittle silence that hung like a tangible curtain between them.

Luke looked up, his sea-green eyes murkey and serious. I wish I knew what he was thinking, thought Naomi, feeling even more nervous. His great bulk filled the small hallway, his very presence making the room shrink.

'Ready?' he asked briefly.

'Yes.'

There was no need to ask if he had told Sister Murphy that she wouldn't be in, he would have made all the necessary arrangements. Naomi knew him well enough by now to know that he would have left nothing to chance. Without another word she followed him down the path, and climbed into the car. Equally silent, Luke took his place beside her, and they started on their journey.

Time and time again Naomi opened her mouth to say something but then closed it again. Luke for his part seemed quite content to remain silent. Although Naomi felt it wasn't a particularly cheerful silence, and the expression on his face hardly encouraged her to rush into conversation.

Finally, however, she did pluck up the courage to speak. 'Has Dirk said anything to you?' she asked timidly. 'About me, I mean.'

'No,' came the abrupt, monosyllabic reply.

'Oh, I thought perhaps . . .' Diffidently she fumbled for the right words. Uncomfortably she fidgeted and, out of force of habit, slipped her feet out of the new shoes she was wearing.

Luke glanced down, and realising what she'd done, Naomi hastily stuffed her feet back into the shoes, expecting a sarcastic comment. But all he said was. 'I shall leave you and Dirk together for your heart-to-heart.' Seeing her worried expression he added brusquely. 'You needn't concern yourself—I'm not going to hang around and eavesdrop. But please make sure that between the pair of you, you get something worked out. I want to see you *both* happy and settled, and a good future planned for Toby.'

'But Dirk and I . . .'

'I'm not interested in explanations. As you told me once before, it's your business, not mine.' The cold expressionless finality in Luke's voice kept Naomi silent for the rest of the journey.

He'd like to see them both happy, that was a laugh! Perhaps he thought that she and Dirk were going to fall into each other's arms, and that everything would be happy ever after. Maybe that was what he'd meant by his comments the night before, about everything turning out all right. It made the reality all the more bitter, all the more hard to accept.

The only future Naomi could see was a bleak and empty one—a future without Toby, and certainly no future with the man sitting beside her. In the cold light of day, her dreams of Luke even liking her were laughable. It was quite plain, written all over his face in fact, that he wasn't the slightest bit interested in her. He was only too anxious to see her settled with Dirk. The attraction she had felt between them had clearly been a product of her own over-active imagination.

When they arrived at the hospital, she was led to Dirk's room. He lay waiting anxiously for her arrival, still swathed in bandages, but conscious and alert.

'I'll leave,' said Luke briefly, and was gone before either she or Dirk could speak.

But by the end of the morning, however, and much to her surprise, Naomi was feeling a good deal happier. A great weight had been lifted from her shoulders.

Although she had never admitted it, not even to Aunt Flo, the secret of Toby's birth had been a burden over the years. Now at last the truth was out, and it was not only Dirk who had learned the truth. Naomi too had learned the reason he had never contacted her. Her sister Tiffany had not told anyone, not even Dirk, her surname. She had always teased Dirk by telling him she wanted to be the mysterious woman in his life.

'She was certainly that all right,' Dirk had said sadly. 'If only she had trusted me!' Naomi felt a sudden surge of compassion for him.

He told her that he loved Tiffany, but she had never wanted to even consider settling down, preferring her erratic lifestyle, always on the move. Even the model agency hadn't known her surname—to them she was just Tiffany. When she had disappeared it seemed as if she had vanished into thin air. No trace of her could be found.

Suddenly Naomi realised the pieces of the jigsaw fitted. Tiffany had disappeared to Wales to have her baby, intending to have him adopted; but instead she had died, and Naomi had arrived and adopted Toby herself.

The only blot on the horizon, as far as Naomi was concerned, was the future of Toby. They both agreed that he would have to be told the story of his parentage, but later, when he was a little older and would be able to understand. In the meantime Dirk, not unnaturally, wanted a say in the future of his son. One thing he did make clear to Naomi was that he felt he should be brought up in a family with a man in it, and not an all-female household.

'We won't rush into anything,' he told Naomi, 'but we must consider what's the best for Toby in the long term.'

Although Naomi agreed with his sentiments, the practicality was another matter. She didn't feel Toby's life should be disrupted with strangers, and Dirk had told her he couldn't possibly have him. He had several more years of his racing contract to run, which meant travelling the world, and what was more to point, as he pointed out to Naomi, he didn't have a wife.

Naomi gave a ruefule smile at his last remark. 'Your dear brother,' she said, carefully keeping her voice on an even keel, 'thinks you and I were lovers. He thinks Toby is my child, and I also have the feeling that he fondly imagines we'll be tying the matrimonial knot for Toby's sake in the very near future.'

Dirk snorted with laughter. 'Luke's like that. He's old-fashioned in many ways.' Then he added with an engaging grin, 'Why didn't you enlighten him?'

Naomi found herself smiling back. Dirk's boyish, irrascible charm was hard to resist at close quarters. She found herself thinking how much nicer he had grown since she'd last met him. But of course, that had been more than eight years ago, and he had matured since then.

'Well?' Dirk repeated the question.

Naomi pulled a face. 'Perverseness, I suppose, partly, and the fact that Luke didn't give me chance to get a word in edgeways,' she said, 'and anyway, he always makes me so nervous!'

'Oh, really? But I thought Luke and . . .' Dirk's voice trailed off thoughtfully, then he added briskly, as if he had made a sudden decision, 'I'll work something out for Toby that will meet with your approval, you see if I don't.' He took her hand and squeezed it vigorously, smiling broadly.

'I'm sure you will,' Naomi tried to smile back, at the same time valiantly battling to keep the tremble from her voice as she returned the pressure of his hand.

Dirk and Luke, two brothers and so alike in so many ways, particularly in their supreme self-confidence that they could work everything out. She had no doubt whatsoever that between them they *would* work everything out for Toby, and that it would be something she couldn't possibly disapprove of. But where exactly would that leave her?

As if to confirm her fears, when she eventually left Dirk's room, Luke was waiting outside with a man she had never seen before.

'This is Charles,' he said abruptly, 'a member of Dirk's team. He'll be driving you back to Longstone. I have business to attend to here.'

Naomi stared at him with apprehension. 'If it's about Toby . . .' she began.

'Nothing that need concern you yet,' came the reply. He nodded to Charles. 'Deliver her safely.'

Naomi turned away, her amber-flecked eyes brimming with unshed tears. A sixth sense told her it *was* to do with Toby's future, and already she was being excluded.

Disconsolately wandering alone along the edge of the foreshore of the saltings, she eventually perched aimlessly on the ancient wooden stile straddling the path that led to the mill at Maltsworth. The tide was out, exposing the sand and mud seething now with wild birds. Waders of every description sifted through the seaweed for morsels of food, but today the familiar beauty didn't touch her as it usually did. Wild birds strutted quite close to her feet, but remained unseen; her mind was on the future. What would it hold for her?

'Why didn't you tell me about Tiffany?'

The voice from behind startled her. Unknown to her Luke had walked silently along the springy turf edging the foreshore, and now joined her sitting on the old wooden stile.

'Well, I . . .'

'You purposely let me think Toby was your child all along, and then still didn't deny it even after we'd met Dirk.' His tone was accusing, his eyes narrowed against the evening sun flashed with what Naomi could only presume to be anger.

A reflection flashed in her own eyes, lighting the amber flecks with a burning gold. 'Because you always did just what you're doing now,' she retaliated. 'You jumped to conclusions—your own conclusions. You were never interested in hearing my story. Even this morning, when I tried to tell you, you shut me up. *I'm not interested,* you said.'

She turned and gazed with unseeing eyes across the flat expanse of the saltings, now shot with soft purples and pinks reflecting the dying rays of the sun. 'Anyway,' she added, 'perhaps I did let you think it at the beginning, but I didn't care then because it was none of your business. It was only later that I . . .'

'You didn't care?' he interrupted loudly. 'You didn't care what I thought?'

'Yes, no . . . I mean of course I *did* care that you obviously thought the worst of me, and my pride was hurt. But I had, and always will have, a loyalty to Tiffany. By insulting me, you insulted her.'

'You're ridiculous, do you know that?' Shaken, Naomi looked at the black scowl on his face. This was turning out to be much worse than she had ever thought possible. Would he ever begin to understand?

Taking a deep breath, she stuck to her guns and continued. 'And then when we met Dirk, by then explanations were out of the question.'

'Why, for heaven's sake?' Luke sounded more exasperated by the minute.

'Because of the accident, because you said that if Dirk died it would be my fault.' She paused, and added in a low voice, 'And in a way it would have been.' She turned away. 'Now please go. I don't want to know what you and Dirk have in mind for Toby—not yet, anyway. I've got to come to terms with losing him. Just go away and leave me in peace. Tonight I want to be alone. I've had enough of the Roderick brothers for one day!'

Luke's distinctive ringing laugh echoed out across the silent seascape, causing a flock of seagulls to take flight in surprise, screaming their disapproval as they swept overhead . . . 'I suppose I should be thankful you didn't say you'd had enough of us to last a lifetime,' he said.

'Get lost, and don't joke, I'm not in the mood,' snapped Naomi. How could he be so insensitive?

'That sounds a little more like the Naomi I've grown to know and love.'

Startled, she swivelled her head to look at him.

His dark saturnine face suddenly flashed with a wicked smile that turned her legs to jelly, and before she had time to draw a breath, long arms reached out and pulled her close.

'We have a lot of talking to do, you and I,' he said huskily, 'but it can wait for a moment.'

'But . . .'

'I said it can wait,' he repeated deliberately. 'We've more important things to do.'

As his warm mouth closed possessively over hers, Naomi wondered hazily if she was dreaming. But the very real pressure of his mouth on her lips, and the rippling threads of fire that quivered through her body, convinced her that they were on earth—feelings reinforced by the fact that they appeared to be in imminent danger of falling off the stile.

Luke evidently thought so too. 'We'll be more comfortable here,' he said persuasively, pulling her down on the sweet smelling turf, studded with daises and the heavy nodding heads of pink clover.

Only the seabirds wheeling in the purple vaulting sky saw Luke raining kisses down on Naomi's face. His lips tenderly traced the delicate line of her throat, down to where the swell of her breasts was exposed by the open neck of her blouse.

Naomi forgot everything in the pleasure of the moment. I oughtn't to succumb so easily, she thought vaguely, but resistance was beyond her. No man had ever ignited her mind and body with such a burning flame of desire as Luke could. With just the touch of his hands and mouth, he released the pent-up feelings she had tried so hard to bury. As they surfaced, she found herself hungrily returning his kisses, moving her body in unknowing sensuality against his.

At last Luke drew back, and raising his head gazed down at her. Wonderingly she tentatively traced the outline of his determined jawline with her finger-tips.

'I love you.' It was a simple direct statement, but his voice was ragged with emotion. 'I think I've loved you since the first day your golden eyes blazed defiance at me.' He bent down and kissed her lingeringly, then whispered into the warm corner of her mouth, 'I have to confess I was beside myself with jealousy when I thought you were the girl Dirk had been grieving over for the past eight years. But whatever the reason, I should never have said those terrible things to you—it was wrong of me. Can you ever forgive me?'

'There's nothing to forgive, because I love you too.' Naomi heard a voice she hardly recognised as her own whispering back.

'Let's go to the mill.' Luke pulled her up to her feet and swiftly began to button up her blouse.

'But Matt . . .'

'Matt won't be there.'

'But he might not like us . . .'

Luke effectively silenced her by kissing her protesting mouth and then the tip of her nose. 'There you go again! But, but, but, I've never know a woman object so much! Matt won't mind, because the mill doesn't belong to him, it belongs to me. He was just keeping an eye on it until I could move in.'

'It belongs to you? But why didn't you tell me?'

'Because it didn't take me very long to find out that you were one of the most obstinate creatures to walk this earth. And I had more than a shrewd suspicion that you'd find some very good reasons for not coming to the mill if you knew it belonged to me.' He started kissing her again, starting at the side of her neck and working upwards until his teeth were gently tugging at her earlobe.

Naomi felt her head beginning to spin. She couldn't keep up with events, everything was happening too fast. 'Stop it!' she said, pushing Luke firmly away. 'I can't think properly when you're kissing me.'

'I prefer you not thinking properly.' Resolutely Luke pulled her back within the circle of his arms.

'Don't think,' he murmured. 'give in to your
instincts. I want you, and I know you want me too.
Every kiss, every touch tells me so.'

Naomi tried to summon her scattered wits. 'I'm
not . . . I'm not as sexually experienced as you
think.' she whispered, shyness suddenly
overwhelming her, 'and I'm not—I can't . . .'

'Be a one-night stand?' Luke asked gently,
putting a finger under her chin and tipping her face
up towards him.

Naomi nodded, her cheeks stained pink with
embarrassment.

'It wasn't a one-night stand I had in mind,' he
said slowly, 'more like an *every-night* stand.'

'But . . .'

He laughed teasing. 'Here we go again! You
sound like an outboard motor having difficulty in
starting!'

'I am having difficulty,' confessed Naomi,
'difficulty in understanding.' She could hardly
believe her ears. Every night! Did he mean——?
No, it couldn't possibly be . . .

The dark shape of the mill suddenly loomed
ahead of them, startling her. They must have been
walking in that direction all the time, and she
hadn't even been aware of it.

Silently Luke unlatched the gate and ushered her
inside, then fastening the gate firmly, he turned to
her and sighed. 'I can see I'm going to have to do it
properly,' he said, dropping to his knees in the
loose gravel of the path leading to the doorway.

Although she couldn't see the expression on his

face in the deepening dusk, Naomi could tell that he was smiling. 'Will you marry me?' he said. 'And before you say "but", you ought to know that I've already told Toby he'll be living at the mill with you and me; and Aunt Flo is busy planning how she's going to reorganise the extra space at the cottage.'

'Well!' Naomi found her voice. 'Of all the nerve—you don't even know whether I'll say yes!'

Luke got to his feet and swung open the heavy-timbered tarred door leading into the mill. 'I've got all night to help you make up your mind,' he said, kicking the door shut behind her, and pulling her roughly into his arms.

'The trouble with you,' said Naomi, feeling she ought to put up at least a token of resistance, but having difficulty speaking between kisses, 'is that you're too used to getting your own way.'

'Do I take it that I *am* going to get my own way?'

'Well . . . I suppose——oh, Luke!' Suddenly Naomi threw all caution to the winds and began to kiss him back passionately.

'Good,' murmured Luke 'I'm glad you've made up your mind, darling. But first sit down. I intend to start as I mean to go on.'

Before she had time to even gasp a 'but', Naomi found herself plonked down very firmly in the wickerwork armchair that stood beside the window. Without another word Luke bent down and pulled off her shoes, and leaning out of the open window threw them one after the other as

far as he could out into the soft mud of the
saltings. A faint plop echoed as each shoe landed.

'But they were new!' wailed Naomi, jumping up
and peering out into the gathering darkness.

'I suppose you could always go and get them if
you feel that strongly,' said Luke, laughter running
through his voice. 'Although I did have it in mind
to buy you a whole new set of shoes, a size *larger*.'

'Oh, Luke!' Naomi began to laugh. 'Then you
don't mind my big feet?'

'I've always thought big feet are very sexy,' said
Luke seriously. 'That was another thing I noticed
about you.' He swung her up into his arms and
started to carry her up the winding stairs.

'This is ridiculous conversation, do you know
that?' she sighed, nestling her head into the curve
of his shoulder. 'We have so many sensible things
we ought to be discussing, there are so many things
I'm not sure about.'

'First things first,' answered Luke, a faint
tremor in his voice as he gently lowered her down
on to the huge soft bed. He ran his hands slowly
down the length of her body, the touch of his
fingers sending shooting quivers of desire deep
down into the pit of her stomach. 'By the morning,
darling,' he whispered hoarsely, 'I promise you
won't have a doubt left in your head.' As he spoke
he deftly slipped off her blouse and, unclipping her
bra, cupped the small mound of her breasts in his
hands. 'Perfect,' he murmured, bending to touch
the rosy tips of her nipples lightly with his tongue.
Naomi relaxed, as a sensuous feeling of lethargy

stole over her. Slowly Luke lowered himself on to the bed beside her, and then sliding down began to shower her feet with a thousand flickering kisses.

'I think I'll begin by convincing you that I meant what I said about sexy feet!'

HOW FAR CAN LOVE BE CHALLENGED

REDWOOD EMPIRE *By Elizabeth Lowell*   £2.9

The best-selling author of *'Tell Me No Lies'*, creates a bitter triangle of lov
and hate amidst the majestic wilderness of America's Northwest empir
19-year old Maya Charter's marriage to Hale Hawthorne is jeopardized b
her lingering feelings for her former lover – his son, Will.

CHERISH THIS MOMENT *By Sandra Canfield*   £2.7

Senator Cole Damon is Washington's most eligible bachelor, but h
attraction to journalist Tracy Kent is hampered by her shocking past.
their love is to survive, he must first overcome her fear of betrayal.

BEYOND COMPARE *By Risa Kirk*   £2.5

When T.V. presenters Dinah Blake and Neil Kerrigan meet to co-host
special programme, the only thing they have in common is their growin
attraction for each other. Can they settle their differences, or is the
conflict a recipe for disaster?

These three new titles will be out in bookshops from March 1989.

W❂RLDWIDE

Available from Boots, Martins, John Menzies, W.H. Smith, Woolworths and
other paperback stockists.

A Mother's Day gift that will last longer than Flowers

MAN OF THE HIGH PLAINS – *Kerry Allyne*
BITTERSWEET HONEYMOON – *Marjorie Lewty*
SHADES OF YESTERDAY – *Leigh Michaels*
PARADISE FOR TWO – *Betty Neels*

Four favourite authors in an exquisite gift pack. There's no better way to show your mother you love her ... or you can even treat yourself!

Available from January 1989. Price £5.00

From: Boots, Martins, John Menzies, W H Smith, Woolworths and other paperback stockists.

Doctor Nurse Romances

Romance in modern medical life

Read more about the lives and loves of doctors and nurses in the fascinatingly different backgrounds of contemporary medicine. These are the three Doctor Nurse romances to look out for next month.

DR DRUMMOND ADVISES
Grace Read

MOUNTAIN CLINIC
Jennifer Eden

SURGEON IN THE HIGHLANDS
Drusilla Douglas

Buy them from your usual paperback stockist, or write to: Mills & Boon Reader Service, P.O. Box 236, Thornton Rd, Croydon, Surrey CR9 3RU, England. Readers in Southern Africa — write to: Independent Book Services Pty, Postbag X3010, Randburg, 2125, S. Africa.

Mills & Boon
the rose of romance

Mills & Boon

WINTER COMPETITION

How would you like a
year's supply of Mills & Boon Romances ABSOLUTELY FREE?
Well, you can win them! All you have to do is complete the word
puzzle below and send it into us by 30th June 1989.
The first five correct entries picked out of the bag after that date
will each win a year's supply of Mills & Boon Romances (Ten
books every month - **worth over £100!**) What could be easier?

C	W	A	E	T	A	N	R	E	B	I	H
H	R	I	C	E	R	W	O	L	G	M	Y
I	F	R	O	S	T	A	O	E	L	U	Y
L	N	I	B	O	R	U	D	R	I	V	Y
L	B	L	E	A	K	B	W	I	I	N	F
T	O	G	L	O	V	E	S	E	A	R	R
S	O	S	G	O	L	R	W	I	E	T	E
T	T	C	H	F	I	R	E	L	R	O	E
S	K	A	T	E	M	Y	C	I	K	S	Z
I	Y	R	R	E	M	I	P	I	N	E	E
N	A	F	D	E	C	E	M	B	E	R	N
N	C	E	M	I	S	T	L	E	T	O	E

Ivy	Radiate	December	Star	Merry
Frost	Chill	Skate	Ski	Pine
Bleak	Glow	Mistletoe	Inn	
Boot	Ice	Fire		
Robin	Hibernate	Log		**PLEASE TURN**
Yule	Icicle	Scarf		**OVER FOR**
Freeze	Gloves	Berry		**DETAILS**
				ON HOW
				TO ENTER

How to enter

All the words listed overleaf, below the word puzzle, are hidden in the grid. You can find them by reading the letters forwards, backwards, up or down, or diagonally. When you find a word, circle it, or put a line through it. After you have found all the words the remaining letters (which you can read from left to right, from the top of the puzzle through to the bottom) will spell a secret message.

Don't forget to fill in your name and address in the space provided and pop this page in an envelope (you don't need a stamp) and post it today. Hurry - competition ends 30th June 1989

Only one entry per household please.

Mills & Boon Competition,
FREEPOST,
P.O. Box 236,
Croydon,
Surrey CR9 9EL.

Secret message _____

_____

Name_____

Address_____

_____

_____

_____Postcode_____

COMP5